Visit us at www.boldstrokesbooks.com

By the Author

Harmony

Worth the Risk

Sea Glass Inn

Improvisation

Mounting Danger

Wingspan

Blindsided

Mounting Evidence

Love on Tap

Tales from Sea Glass Inn

Amounting to Nothing

You Make Me Tremble

You Make
Me Tremble

by
Karis Walsh

2017

ISBN 13: 978-1-62639-901-3

This Trade Paperback Original Is Published By
Bold Strokes Books, Inc.
P.O. Box 249
Valley Falls, NY 12185

First Edition: July 2017

CREDITS

Editor: Ruth Sternglantz
Production Design: Susan Ramundo
Cover Design By Sheri (graphicartist2020@hotmail.com)

CHAPTER ONE

Casey Radnor put her book down and climbed out of the Tundra. She had been waiting in line for a ferry for over three hours now. Before the first cancellation, she had sat in her truck while the line inched forward maddeningly every so often as the people in front of her anticipated the expected ferry and closed gaps between cars. During the second hour, she had occasionally moved forward an entire car length because some people gave up and left the line. Now, with the announcement of yet another cancellation, she figured pacing around the ferry dock would be more productive than sitting inside the truck and pretending to read.

Casey had lived in Seattle long enough to have idled in many a ferry line. Usually, however, she had to wait because so many people were trying to escape to the Olympic Peninsula and the ferries' expansive bellies couldn't accommodate them all. Not the case here at the Anacortes terminal. Only twenty or so vehicles were queued up in the holding area, and Casey assumed this was highly unusual for such a beautiful fall Friday. Hordes of tourists should be here, vying for spots on the ferry and snapping photos of the scenery. Instead, most people remained huddled in their cars as they waited for a ferry that might never come. Casey was sure it would be full when it arrived—*if* it arrived—of those who wanted to escape the earthquake-damaged San Juan Islands.

Her hand shook as she used the key remote to lock her truck. Not that she had anything valuable in the cab worth stealing. A few clothes—mostly in need of a wash after her trip to the Bay Area. A couple paperbacks and a small toiletries case. No one looking at her dinged and scratched truck with its messy cab would expect the old aluminum truck box in the bed to contain thousands of dollars' worth of equipment, but just one device from the selection she had in there cost more than her truck and the cars in front and behind her combined.

A salty breeze tossed her short reddish-brown hair into her eyes as she walked across the paved parking lot and toward the pier. She had meant to get a haircut before speaking at the conference at Stanford, her alma mater, earlier in the week, but her new job at the University of Washington seismology lab had kept her too busy to even think about personal vanity. She had spent most of her speech self-consciously pushing her hair across her forehead. Any hope of getting it cut once she returned home had been destroyed when the earthquake struck.

Casey rubbed suddenly sweaty palms on her jeans. People usually assumed that earthquakes didn't bother her at all, probably because she had chosen to study them as her life's work and because she could get admittedly carried away when she started talking about transpressional faulting and subduction quakes. But when a real earthquake struck, she was as scared and helpless as everyone else in the area. Her fear might be camouflaged somewhat by her scientific curiosity and hidden behind a driving desire to help people learn to anticipate and survive significant seismic activity, but it was real nonetheless. Years of schooling and work hadn't made her immune to the sense of panic that gripped her when her plane had shimmied across the tarmac yesterday.

She left the paved lot, and smooth, large rocks rolled under her feet as she walked down a slope and toward the water. The stones got progressively smaller as she got closer to the waves lapping against the shore, but they never gave way to sand. Normally, Casey would be sifting through the rocks in search of some non-indigenous specimen or an imprint of a fossilized shell, but today she couldn't focus on the details of the rocky beach. She chose a flat, gray oval and flicked her wrist as she tried to skip it across the surface of Puget Sound. It disappeared with a heavy splash on the first bounce.

Casey sighed and looked for another skipping stone. The rocks under her feet shifted again, and she almost lost her balance. *Aftershock?* No. She regained her balance, calmed her breathing, and tossed another flat stone into the water with a non-skipping plop. She had been tense on the flight yesterday, even before the quake hit, and the sudden lurching motion had made every muscle seize. The pilot had been taxiing to the terminal, and most of the passengers—Casey included—had ignored the lit seat belt sign and unbuckled as they prepared to deplane. What could possibly happen on the ground? Casey of all people should have known the answer to that question. Instead, she had been one of the people tossed into the aisleway as the plane had lurched to the side, one set of landing gear buckling under the weight of the aircraft and throwing people and heavy carry-ons to the side.

If she had a sense of humor about earthquakes, she might have wryly decided that the plane ride had been a fitting end to a lousy week, but she couldn't let herself take such a violent phenomenon lightly. Still, her time at Stanford had sucked.

Running into not one, but two ex-girlfriends in the span of one day? Definitely unpleasant. She shouldn't have been too surprised—not because she had hordes of exes in every city along the West Coast, but because she knew both women were still at the university. One was an applied mathematics professor, and the other was working on yet another doctorate.

Sophie, who collected degrees like some people collected stamps, had been arm in arm with her new girlfriend when Casey ran across her in the bookstore. She had looked at Casey with something suspiciously resembling pity as she asked how she was, if she was seeing anybody, and how well she had been sleeping lately. New girlfriend hadn't seemed fazed by the conversation, no doubt familiar with and attracted to Sophie's nurturing ways. Casey had been, too, when they had first started dating, but she had been at a loss how to respond to so much attention, and unsure of her ability to reciprocate. Besides, she had guessed it was only a matter of time before Sophie's attentions grew less intense.

After the drawn-out breakup with Sophie, Casey had re-examined her dating philosophy. Relationships should be a meeting of minds between two people who respected each other and shared the values of seeking knowledge, working for a higher purpose, and being independent. Math professor Shelby had fit that description perfectly, and their relationship had been about as much fun as it sounded. They had parted ways easily, in a sterile and mutually agreed-upon fashion, and Casey had been left with no real direction for the future except for a resolution to never again date a woman whose name began with *S*.

The green-and-white ferry appeared on the horizon, thankfully bringing Casey out of her memories and back to the present. She turned her back on the view of the Sound, with its patchwork of hilly, fir tree covered islands, and walked back to the ferry line. Part of her recognized how gorgeous the setting was, but most of her longed to be back in the city where people and cultural options filled in the gaps when she wasn't busy at work. Here, she could only focus on the fascinating geological formations surrounding her for so long before the quiet beauty of the place invited self-reflection and contemplation. She needed to get to San Juan, the largest island and namesake of the San Juan Islands archipelago, and get busy with her instruments and notepads.

She had been strangely relieved when her boss had called before she'd even reached the airport parking lot and asked her to go to the islands, close to the epicenter of the earthquake. She had been prepared to get right to the lab and begin examining the loads of data that must have been coming in since the quake, but he wanted her on the island with minimal instruments. She knew this was an audition of sorts. She already had the job at the lab, of course, but her observations and performance when alone in the field would tell him a lot about her. This was her chance to prove her worth—anyone could be trained to read the information provided by high-tech instruments, but not everyone had the instincts and intuition to interpret clues without them. She had gone straight from the airport to the university lab where she picked up the portable gear she would need for the trip.

She had seen evidence of the earthquake's magnitude as she inched through the city traffic. Closed roads, buildings with whole sections sheared off, emergency vehicles on every street. Even out here, where most of the rural areas seemed untouched on the surface, her practiced eye recognized the pattern of fallen trees, and she was able to guess which ones had recently come down and which were unrelated to the earthquake. She hadn't bothered to return to her apartment, though, to assess the damage to her own space. She didn't have much to lose. She had a few geodes she had collected, and those would survive a fall from a shelf. Her filing cabinets might have fallen over, but her books and papers—the main objects she cared about—were probably fine. Once she had made sure her local friends were okay, she had been left without anything else to worry about except doing her job to help make the future safer. She saw other people frantic about lost homes and belongings, and she wanted to do what she could to prevent more damage when the next quake hit.

She got back to the truck and double-checked the instruments in the box before settling in the driver's seat and putting on her seat belt. The slow-moving ferry was still a distant speck on the horizon, but she was ready to get on board and get to her destination. She drummed her fingers on the steering wheel for several minutes before taking out her notepad. She had already made notes about the damage she had witnessed on her drive from Seattle to Anacortes while she sat in her cheap hotel room last night. The blaring television and her rapid scribbling had calmed her mind enough to let her eventually fall asleep. Now she let her fingers capture what she observed at the ferry landing.

Except for the older trees that had fallen, there was little out here to indicate that a 7.2 magnitude earthquake had occurred the day before. She wasn't much of an artist, but she had needed to learn the basics for her job, and she drew the small wooden terminal and the cars idling beside and in front of her. She drew a series of sketches of the ferry as it approached and docked. She was just penciling in the name of the ferry—the *Klahowya*—when the first vehicles began to disembark.

As she had expected, the ferry was full because of the destruction on the islands and the canceled routes from earlier in the day. Once the vehicles—she counted eighty-six—had been cleared, she and another twenty-three cars filed on board in their place. She considered waiting in the truck with her instruments since the trip would take less than two hours, even with stops at Lopez and Orcas Islands, but she hadn't eaten since dinner the night before. She scrounged in the truck's console for change for the vending machines, checked the lock on the instrument box yet again, and climbed the narrow stairwell to the passenger deck. She sat inside while she ate her barbecue potato chips and drank a Coke, and then she pushed through the door leading to the observation deck.

A blast of chilly autumn wind struck her, and she leaned in to it as she walked toward the bow and rested against the railing. She brushed her bangs out of her eyes again. She was going to have to buy a pair of scissors and cut her own damned hair once she got to Friday Harbor.

Gulls swooped alongside the ferry as the craft made slow progress toward their first stop at Lopez Island. Casey noticed a few seals that occasionally popped to the surface and watched the ferry slide by. She saw fins break the surface now and again. Too small to be whales. Dolphins? Porpoises? She had only taken the bare minimum of biology classes, so she wasn't sure. She occupied her time by counting them instead of identifying. Eleven fins spotted during the forty-two-minute trip to Lopez.

Once there, she watched three cars drive off the ferry and down the two-lane road leading away from the dock and to the rest of the sparsely inhabited island. A tiny terminal and a log-cabin-style convenience store were the only signs of habitation. Casey hoped the town of Friday Harbor, her destination on the more populated San Juan Island, would be more active and lively, but she knew better than to expect a bustling metropolis anywhere out here. Her attention shifted from the miniature ferry landing to the towering fir trees to her still-grumbling stomach before coming to rest on one of the few walk-on passengers.

A seismic reaction. Casey usually was strong enough to resist them, but this one caught her with the same force as the Sound's heavy wind current.

The woman paused before walking up the ramp and squinted up at the ferry, seeming to pick Casey out of the small crowd. She was pretty, in a windswept, wild way. Her gold-brown hair was caught in a ponytail, but several strands were loose and wisping across her face. Her face was as carefully sculpted as if an artist had labored long and hard over every detail. Her expression seemed weary, but that might be more attributable to the animals currently pulling her in different directions. And her body...

Casey sighed and moved away from the railing. The woman was a walk-on, meaning she was probably a local. And she had at least three dogs with her, maybe another one in the small pet crate she carried. Casey wasn't an animal person and she wasn't looking for a date. She headed back toward the vending machines. Chocolate. That's what she needed.

Chapter Two

Iris Mallery stepped over a leash before the Chihuahua on the other end could pull it tight and trip her. An identical small dog was lashed to her wrist with a makeshift leash made of rope, and a German shepherd mix tugged her mercilessly along. A small crate, complete with pregnant cat, was heavy in her other hand. She had started the day wearing a fisherman's knit sweater under a bulky jacket, hoping to fight off the biting wind, but now she wished she had worn something lighter. The shepherd stubbornly wanted to go in the opposite direction, no matter where she was headed, and the matched set of Chihuahuas were intent on running in circles. Iris didn't see any opportunity in the foreseeable future for her to remove one of her warm layers. She hadn't expected such a workout since she had only come to Lopez to pick up the two tiny dogs.

She was tempted by the elevator that would take her to the passenger deck, but the other walk-ons had the same idea and were waiting in line for it. Besides, she wasn't sure how her charges would react to a shifting, shuddering ride in an enclosed box. She wasn't especially keen on the idea, either, since she was still jumpy from the day before. Even being in Agatha's car this morning, on the way to the ferry landing, had made her anxious. She needed open spaces and fresh air, and the best route was the wooden staircase. It was barely wide enough for her, let alone three meandering dogs and a plastic crate, but she climbed one step at a time. She couldn't risk tripping and falling backward with all four animals. Luckily, no one was on the stairs going in the opposite direction, and she finally made it to the passenger deck. She paused for a few seconds, breathing hard from the steep climb with her charges, and then struggled to open the heavy glass door leading to the outer deck.

She and her pack emerged onto the deck just as the ferry began to churn out of the slip. The sudden movement, combined with the small crowd of people who were settling into positions at the rail and the chilly gust of wind shuddering through the evergreen trees, startled the dogs. Their agitation increased, and Iris felt the rope connecting her to the shepherd slipping out of her grasp. She dove toward the end of the leash as it disappeared between passengers.

"Damn," she said, shifting the crate into a better position and setting off after the wayward dog. She jostled around people until she got to the stern. Despite the chaos, a sudden sense of peace dropped over her as she rounded the back corner of the glassed-in portion of the deck where she was sheltered from the wind and from most of the other passengers. She saw the dog trotting toward one of the few people back here—the woman Iris had briefly noticed while she was boarding the ferry. The woman looked surprised to see the loose dog, and she tucked a candy bar into the pocket of her jacket before reaching down and grabbing his trailing rope. She glanced around until she saw Iris standing a few yards away. Iris tried to gather her roaming thoughts and her rambunctious dogs before she walked over to the woman and dog.

"Missing someone?"

Iris smiled in response, unable to resist. The woman standing in front of her was even more stunning up close than she had been from a distance. Her short hair shone with myriad shades of red and brown, and her blue-gray eyes seemed born from the sky and water around them. She held the rope awkwardly in one hand—in contrast to her otherwise confident bearing—and she used the other to swipe her long bangs out of her eyes. Her jeans and jacket displayed expensive urban labels, but they looked rugged and lived in. Iris could picture her humbly posing for a picture at the top of Everest or Kilimanjaro, or some other trek-worthy destination. If Iris had been here in any other situation, she would have been wildly attracted to her. As it was, however, she felt too out of sorts to even consider trying to meet someone new. What kind of conversation could they have while she was chasing wayward dogs? Too bad the circumstances weren't different...

Iris sighed. Who was she kidding? Even without the dogs and cat, she wouldn't have been brave enough to chat up some stranger on the ferry. Especially one who managed to make her feel the heady combination of breathlessness and peace.

"Yes, thank you," she said, reaching for the shepherd's rope. "He got scared by the wind and the crowds."

Iris paused while they both looked around. She could almost read the question on the woman's face. *Crowds?* At the moment, they were the only two people near the stern.

Iris laughed briefly, and then stopped. The sound seemed foreign to her even though the day before yesterday had been filled with hilarity as she and her rescue team played with their newest residents, a pair of baby goats. One day and one earthquake later, and Iris felt a jolt of guilt that she was able to smile and laugh. "He's been loose in the woods since the quake yesterday, and he lives on Lopez, so ten people are a huge crowd to him. Thank you for catching him."

"You're welcome. I'm Casey. I'd shake your hand, but you don't seem to have a free one. Do you always travel with all your pets?"

"I'm Iris." She put the carrier on the ground next to her and shook Casey's hand as the cat inside the small crate let out a deep yowl. Iris bent down and picked her up again, hiding the warmth she felt spreading over her face at the simple touch of Casey's hand. She had already realized she was physically attracted to her, and she wouldn't have been surprised by a tingly, arousing reaction from the handshake, but what she felt was unexpected and disconcerting. Calm. Strength. Grounding. Things that had been swept out of Iris's heart when the earthquake shook her world the day before.

"To answer your question, they're not my pets. Not really. They must have gotten loose yesterday, and I'm taking them to the shelter I run in Friday Harbor. The rescue center on Lopez is overcrowded, and they asked me to take a few animals. Do you mind if I sit?" Iris shuffled her milling pack over to a bench and sat down, keeping the crate on her lap.

Only twenty-four hours after the quake, and she was exhausted from the nonstop intake and processing of lost animals. The sheer numbers of them were discouraging—would she be able to reunite all of them with their owners?—and she didn't have any more room to spare than the Lopez center did. But she hadn't been able to say no when asked for help. How could she turn away any of these animals? "I was supposed to take these two Chihuahuas, and I thought they could ride together in the crate. But someone brought in the shepherd while I was there, and another person called about a pregnant cat that was hiding under a broken deck at an empty house."

Iris tilted her head to indicate the carrier, and the cat let out a helpful howl, as if providing testimony for the story. Dozens of displaced animals had already arrived at Iris's shelter, and the cat promised to produce a few more within the next week or two. Somehow Iris would have to house them all, feed them, provide necessary vet care…She reached down to pet the shepherd who had finally settled at her feet and was calmly letting the Chihuahuas wrestle on and around him. She'd manage to take care of these animals, and all the rest that would no doubt be coming to the shelter in the aftermath of the disaster. But right now, she had nothing to do besides sit next to a beautiful woman and share company and conversation with her. She was going to make the most of it.

"Do you live on San Juan?" she asked as the ferry drifted toward the next dock, at Orcas Island. Casey hadn't made a move toward her car yet, so this island obviously wasn't her destination.

"No," Casey said, leaning back on the bench and resting one ankle over her other knee. The casual pose and her soft voice made her seem much more at ease talking to a stranger than Iris normally was. "I live in Seattle. I'm only visiting for a short time."

Iris shook her head. "You picked a hell of a time to come for a vacation. I hope you confirmed your hotel today because a lot of places are closed." *Or you could spend the night with me.*

Iris wasn't sure where the thought had come from. She had been attracted to women before, but never to this extent. How was Casey able to override Iris's residual fear from yesterday and her dread of the upcoming days? Or was she attracted to Casey *because* of yesterday and the resulting sensations of worry and fragility?

Iris wanted to scoot away, to put more inches of space between them, but if she moved, then the dogs would get up and the cat would howl again. She stayed put and tried to ignore the waves of warmth and confidence she felt everywhere her body was close to Casey's. Her hips, her shoulders—damn it, even her elbows—were humming with an awareness of Casey's corresponding body parts.

Casey shrugged, and Iris twitched in response. "I'll find somewhere to stay," Casey said with a surety that Iris didn't think was warranted. "The trip was planned on short notice, so I didn't make a reservation."

Iris hadn't ever traveled to a new town without booking a hotel weeks in advance. And researching restaurants and finding the quickest route to the hospital, just in case. She wasn't the type to leave things to chance. "You'll probably find most tourist places will be closed because of the quake. You won't be able to take any tours, and not many restaurants will be open, and—"

Casey held up her hand. "I understand. I'm used to traveling and sort of following disasters. I'm here to work, anyway, so I won't have time for sightseeing."

"Work," Iris repeated. What kind of job would draw Casey to the shaken San Juans? Iris pictured her shelter, with its damaged kennels and broken fences. "Are you in construction? Because if you are, I'll hire you."

Casey laughed. "No, sorry. I'm here to study the effects of the seismic activity on the islands. The UW lab sent me because the earthquake was caused by a rupture in the Devils Mountain Fault, just off the coast of San Juan Island. It's exciting to have a chance to examine the local area so soon after the earthquake, before repairs are made and the effects are altered."

Casey continued to talk about collecting data and monitoring aftershocks, but Iris stopped listening to the words. Instead, she heard Casey's tone, which betrayed her obvious fascination with seismology and her eagerness to study the island like it was a specimen in a lab.

"So you're here to study us like rats in a maze?" Iris interrupted what might have been a fascinating lecture on seismology if she was heartless and unfeeling. "Do we get a piece of cheese as a reward if we lead you to earthquake damage?"

Casey stared at her for a few seconds, as if stunned to have been pulled out of her earthquake rhapsody. "I'm not here to study you or anybody else," she said with obvious indignation, given her chilly voice and the way she leaned her upper body away from Iris. "This has nothing to do with people."

"It has everything to do with people. People who got hurt and lost their homes and had to close their businesses. And it has everything to do with animals like these who are lost and scared."

Casey held up her hands. Iris didn't interpret the gesture as one of surrender, but as one designed to put physical distance between them, to match the yawning emotional chasm. "The information I can get from this event might help save those animals and businesses next time."

"Event?" Iris shook her head. What a horrible word to use in this context. Disaster would make more sense. Catastrophe. Something to capture the awfulness of those seconds while the earth shuddered. "You make it sound like a family reunion or something. *Event*."

"It's a scientific term," Casey said in clipped tones, "and not meant to imply a cavalier attitude on my part. I didn't cause the earthquake just so I could come study it as a lark. I was sent here to do a job."

Iris felt pain in her temples as she fought off the urge to cry. She looked away from Casey and toward the town of Friday Harbor as the ferry neared the dock. Moored boats filled the harbor, their masts swaying with the movement of the water. Multicolored buildings climbed the hill like steps on a staircase. From this distance, everything seemed normal, if a little quiet. But Iris knew some of the boats had come loose from their moorings and run aground. Quite a few others had smashed into docks and each other. And the buildings, with their stores and restaurants? Most of them were closed, waiting for the town to recover and repair and restore.

"Well, a lot of people on the islands lost their livelihoods yesterday. And most of us have a long uncertain road ahead because our jobs have suddenly gotten much harder. Meanwhile, you'll take some measurements and look at some broken rocks without really seeing the lives that have been damaged."

Casey stood up with a deliberate motion. She seemed to be struggling to retain control. "I'm sorry about these animals," she said gesturing at the dogs and the crate. The Chihuahuas apparently thought she was ready to play with them because they started leaping around her ankles. Iris pulled them back to her, unable to meet Casey's eyes.

"I am also sorry that you have so much work to do because of yesterday. You might not understand the significance of my job, but I do. And it is very important to me. I'll be getting back to it now."

She turned abruptly and startled a seagull that had alighted on the ferry's polished wooden railing. Iris wanted to go after her, but she couldn't match Casey's fast pace with her ragtag menagerie in tow. Besides, what would she say? She had meant every word she'd said, hadn't she? As if she could no longer stay tall without Casey's poised presence beside her, Iris slumped lower on the bench, tired beyond words, and felt the warmth of tears on her face for the first time since the earthquake.

CHAPTER THREE

Casey went back to the vehicle deck and unlocked her truck as the curving arms of Friday Harbor embraced the ferry. She got in and slammed the door shut. Why had she let a complete stranger irritate her? Iris had seen exactly what Casey wanted most people to see—a dispassionate scientist who studied the world around her with a critical and logical mind. Iris, with her leashes and ropes, was wrapped up in the San Juans and in the aftermath of the earthquake while Casey was merely here as an observer, to study the results of seismic activity. She wasn't supposed to get touchy-feely with the locals and their stray dogs.

This was why she liked to keep to herself when she did fieldwork.

Casey scrunched down in her seat and opened a map of the islands. Most people who took this ferry probably pored over maps of tourist attractions and restaurants, but Casey's was a topographic map. No extraneous details about quaint bookstores and souvenir shops. She was here to work. So why was she trying to imagine which of the contour lines crossed Iris's shelter?

She folded the map and put it in her backpack before digging through to see if she had any food left—the chocolate bar she'd practically inhaled hadn't satisfied. She briefly considered eating an old granola bar she found, but she couldn't find an expiration date on the wrapper. She tossed it on the seat beside her and rummaged some more, trying to get Iris's accusing glare out of her mind. Casey had to remain detached from emotions when she was on assignment, but she hadn't felt that way today. The cold touch of the big dog's nose against her palm and the plush softness of his thick fur. The warmth of Iris's hazel eyes and the rich tones of her hair which was as variegated and shiny as polished mahogany. The pang of hunger—having nothing to do with Casey's lack of decent food—that she felt deep in her belly when they had transferred the rough leash between them and their hands touched. Casey felt all those things today, and Iris hadn't noticed. She had only seen the cold and distant exterior. Casey wished Iris had seen more.

She started her truck as they pulled slowly toward the dock. Iris's opinion of her meant nothing. She was here with a purpose, and luckily she was about to be released from the confines of the ferry.

The short line of cars inched slowly over the ramp with a jolt and a clang as each set of tires bumped across the joints. Once they reached the pavement of the terminal parking lot, Casey saw a long zigzag line of vehicles waiting to board. She was momentarily tempted to turn around and join them, but she kept moving with the flow of cars that were leaving the ferry behind.

The town of Friday Harbor was situated on a steep hill that dropped right to the edge of the water. Casey had searched for a hotel and some restaurants while she waited in Anacortes, and to her left she noticed a gray-and-white sign with a picture of a schooner on it and recognized it as one of the places she had been hoping to try. The chef had come here from Los Angeles and had created some sort of Northwest and Thai fusion menu, and Casey had figured a fancy meal or two would fill her time and make her feel like she was still in a big city. The outdoor seating area was glassed in and covered with a bright white canopy, folded to look like an unfurling sail. Unfortunately, a handwritten *Closed for Repairs* sign was prominently displayed in the window.

Casey drove up the hill, and the trend continued. The buildings were an eclectic mix of Craftsmans, Victorians, and plain modern boxes. Most were two to three stories high, and they were packed within inches of each other, each containing several shops and eateries. Flower boxes lined the upper-story railings, and banners flew from every lamppost, put there to welcome tourists who were now leaving in droves. Almost every business had a *Closed* sign on the door or in the front window.

How the hell would she occupy her time and her mind here? She could only work in daylight, and the nights were getting longer. She didn't see many options for filling them in this town.

First, she needed a hotel. She had found one online advertising a hot tub and close proximity to the elegant restaurants she had been hoping to visit, although everything in Friday Harbor appeared to be in close proximity to everything else. It was just a block off the main street, and she parked in front and looked at it skeptically. The hotel filled both floors of one of the Victorians, and it seemed freshly painted in a soft beige with teal accents and bright red doors. A bit gaudy for her taste, but the grounds were neat and well-maintained. Hanging baskets with white primroses, some sort of purple flower she didn't recognize, and a medley of autumn-orange marigolds decorated each corner of the building. The neighborhood seemed quiet.

Eerily quiet.

Casey parked in front of the real estate office next door and got out of her car, inhaling an unexpected whiff of smoke that underlaid the heavier scent of brine and seaweed. She didn't bother to bring her backpack out of the truck because she already had a feeling that this hotel—like most of the other businesses—was closed.

The typed sheet of paper taped to the door confirmed her suspicions. She knocked anyway, hoping someone would be there and take pity on her. She didn't mind sleeping among some rubble as long as she had a bed and at least a partial roof over her head.

"Hotel's closed."

Obviously. Casey turned and smiled anyway at the woman who had emerged from the side door of the building on the other side of the hotel. She looked to be in her sixties, with a long gray ponytail, dark blue jeans, and a bulky red sweater. She tossed a white plastic bag in the dumpster wedged between the buildings.

"The owners have gone back to the mainland," she continued, watching Casey with her hands on her hips. "If you're needing a place to say, you might want to do the same thing. It'll be hard to find an open place around here."

Casey shrugged as if indifferent, but her mind was racing as she pictured herself sleeping in the truck and foraging for berries in the woods. "Thanks, but I can't leave. I'm here for work."

"Repair work?" the woman asked, with the same eager look Iris had given her on the ferry when she asked if Casey was in construction. Too bad she barely knew a hammer from a wrench, or she could make a fortune in this town.

"No." Casey paused. Would every local jump all over her if she told the truth about why she was here, or just Iris? "I'm from the UW seismology lab. Here to study the earthquake."

"Seems you people do a lot of studying, but not a lot of predicting."

"Oh. Well. We're trying to get better. That's why I'm here." Casey felt strangely as if she'd been chastised by a teacher for not doing her homework.

"Then you'll need some food before you get started. I'm Jasmine Gray, but everyone calls me Jazz. Come in."

Jazz had the authority-figure act down pat. Casey trailed after her reluctantly and was surprised to find herself standing in the kitchen of a pub. The vague but unmistakable smell of fried food assaulted her as soon as the door closed behind them. She was about to make an excuse to leave and find somewhere less artery-clogging to eat, but her stomach rumbled loudly. She looked around for the entrance to the public dining area. "I'm glad to find an open restaurant," she said, unable to see a clear way out of the kitchen. "I haven't eaten a meal since yesterday."

"I'm not technically open," Jazz said. "I was just making my own lunch and I might as well feed two. Sit."

She pointed at a stool next to the metal island, and Casey sat obediently. Iris should send her new charges here for training—they'd be sitting and speaking and doing tricks before the day was over. Casey wondered how Iris had fared as she disembarked with her pack of dogs and the howling cat. Casey would have willingly helped her move the menagerie to the dock if Iris hadn't sniped at her.

And if she hadn't sniped right back.

Jazz turned to her gigantic black oven and seemed to forget Casey was there as she got to work on their lunches. Casey watched the preparations with half of her attention—she wasn't usually interested in cooking since she had practically grown up on packaged meals and had never gotten out of the habit of using only the microwave and coffeepot in her kitchen. Soon, though, Casey was caught in a web of fascination as Jazz transformed from bossy, nondescript pub owner to something graceful and masterful. She slathered thick slices of white bread—probably homemade given the irregular shape of the loaf and the plain plastic wrapper—with deep-gold butter and put them on the flat grill. Two hefty fillets, the glossy coral color of wild-caught Pacific salmon, joined the sizzling bread. Once the toast was brown, Jazz topped it with mayonnaise, a layer of basil leaves, and the darkly singed salmon.

Casey was nearly drooling when Jazz pulled a basket out of the deep fryer and tipped a pile of homemade potato chips onto a plate next to the sandwich. The scent of dill mingled with the sticky odor of frying oil.

"Eat," Jazz directed, putting the plate in front of her and sitting down with one of her own. She pointed at a small tub of tartar sauce. "Dip the chips in this."

Casey fought the rebellious urge to salute because she was afraid any sign of sarcasm might result in the food being taken away from her. She picked up a chip that was still hot from the oil and dropped it again, wiping her smarting fingers on her napkin. Jazz just shook her head and popped a boiling hot chip in her mouth without flinching. Casey wanted to rise to the challenge, but she picked up the sandwich instead and took a huge bite. The contrast of crispy bread and sharp basil with salmon so tender she barely had to chew it was divine, and she closed her eyes as she swallowed.

She paused for a moment, savoring the taste and trying to figure out why this setting felt familiar to her. The tang of lemon in the mayonnaise, the smell of flavorful food cooking on the stove, and the cozy feeling of eating in the kitchen. She frowned and opened her eyes before she ate more of the sandwich. Her childhood memories were full of meals served in plastic trays, eaten in the living room while she, her father, and his parents watched some documentary or other on television. Casey paused before she put the last bit of sandwich in her mouth.

Her mother, that was it. Standing in the kitchen and making something delicious while a very tiny Casey sat on the counter next to her. Casey swore she could hear the rhythmic tap of her younger self's heels against the cupboard as she swung her legs back and forth and watched her mom chop an herb and add it to a simmering pot of soup.

Casey chewed the rest of her food, but the flavor had disappeared. She had lost her mother when she was only four, and memories of her were few and far between. Casey was never sure if she was glad when they unexpectedly arrived, or if she'd rather they disappeared forever. They always left a gaping hole inside. She hadn't known how to grieve when she was young, and she felt as if she was back in the middle of an unfinished process every time she thought of her mother.

"Do you mind telling me about yesterday?" she asked Jazz as she used a potato chip flecked with bits of dill to scoop up some tartar sauce. She'd do what her grandparents told her to do every time she cried about missing her mom during that first year without her. Work. Pick up a book, solve a puzzle, do some homework—yes, the accelerated school they enrolled her in gave homework in kindergarten. By the second year after her mother's death, Casey had become an expert on refocusing her attention whenever it wandered toward sadness.

"No, I don't mind," Jazz said, setting down the second half of her sandwich and wiping her hands. She stood up and got two Cokes out of the fridge while she talked. "I was serving lunch—we had a big crowd because the weather is warm for this time of year. I was carrying a tray of beers to one of the tables, and everything started to shake. The glasses fell, people were screaming. It takes the brain a few seconds to realize what's going on, you know?"

"I do," Casey nodded. She ate another chip and was relieved to find her sense of taste was functioning again. She washed away the heaviness of the fried food with a swallow of Coke. "I was on a plane taxiing to the terminal. I wasn't sure if we had run over something, or another plane had hit us. What did the motion feel like to you?"

"Violent. Like we were in a carton of orange juice and someone was shaking us real hard." She paused. "I remember a big quake about ten, eleven years ago. I had just moved to the island. That one was different—the earth was rolling like a huge wave had come out of the Sound and was washing over us. It didn't feel as rough as this one, although the damage was still pretty severe. We must have been farther from the epicenter back then, I guess. You'd know better than I."

Casey shook her head. She was picturing Iris and her shelter. She must have been feeling terrified and helpless, with so many animals under her care and no way to protect them until the shaking stopped. "You're right about the epicenter being miles south of here a decade ago, but that isn't what causes the different kind of movement. The rupture in the Devils Mountain Fault was deeper in the earlier earthquake. That'll give you the smoother rolling sensation, even though the magnitude was almost the same as this one."

Jazz leaned forward and stared at her, as if searching for something. "Does it help you? To be so clinical about it, I mean."

Casey crunched on another chip before answering. "No. And yes. It doesn't make me less scared or less in danger when there's an earthquake, but I think I recover faster than other people. Once it's over, I have a job to do, turning something frightening into a collection of data to be studied."

She looked around the kitchen again, thinking about what she had just said. Was it true? Had she bounced back from yesterday's fear and become the cool-headed scientist she was meant to be? She wasn't sure. Would she have been as easily provoked by Iris today if she was completely in control again? Probably. She held most people at a certain distance, but Iris had somehow wedged her way under Casey's skin, touching her where she was too sensitive to handle contact and somehow making her crave even more. She pushed her plate away, her stomach finally full, although her insides still felt hollow.

Casey was accustomed to noticing major damage from the earthquakes she studied. Cracked walls, broken windows, caved-in roofs. She saved her detailed examination for nature, minutely looking at fractures and patterns. But here, in Jazz's kitchen and with Iris's accusations ringing through her head, she saw smaller signs of yesterday's disaster. Tubs of ruined produce, shelves in disarray. One of the refrigerators leaned at an odd angle, obviously broken. Even discounting major damage, Jazz had hours of work ahead of her just to get the kitchen organized and to replace food and dishes that had been lost.

She reached for her wallet. "Lunch was delicious," she said, pulling out a couple of twenties. "I'll be in Friday Harbor for a few days. I'll have to spend a lot of my time on the east side of the island, but I can come by and help you—"

Jazz covered her hand and pushed it away. "You keep your money," she said. "I enjoyed having a little company today.

Come back anytime you need a meal, but don't you worry about me. Those of us who've stayed will be organizing work parties this afternoon. We'll take care of the ones who need the most help first, and then work together to get the rest of the businesses up and running. You just figure out how to let us know in advance next time this is going to happen. The lot of you dropped the ball on this one."

"Sorry," Casey mumbled, apologizing for the entire community of seismologists and the capricious events they studied. She could predict without a doubt that there would be several earthquakes of varying magnitudes over the next month—most too subtle for the average person to notice—and she was sure more high-magnitude seismic events would take place along the Northwest's fault lines in the future. But saying exactly when, exactly where, and exactly how powerful they'd be was far beyond anyone's abilities right now. Soon, she hoped. She would do whatever it took to help make predictions more reliable and accurate.

Jazz gave her hand another pat. "I'd offer you a place to stay, but my little house is a mess. I'm staying with a friend, and he already has a houseful of us refugees. The fire officials are making rounds all the time, otherwise I'd let you sleep in here."

"I'll be fine," Casey said with a confident smile. "There are plenty of hotels and guest houses on the island. One of them is bound to be open, or at least willing to let me have a room for a week or so."

"I'm sure you're right," Jazz said with a nod and a smile, although her expression seemed to say the opposite.

Chapter Four

Iris got out of Agatha's car and reached into the backseat for the shepherd and the cat crate while Agatha retrieved the two Chihuahuas. The old white Buick wasn't as fancy as Iris's sportier little coupe, but it came in handy when they needed to transport animals. Agatha had met the ferry when it arrived, and while they got the dogs and cat situated, Iris had surreptitiously watched Casey drive a big, beat-up Toyota truck past her and into Friday Harbor. Confused by the angry way she had treated Casey—so unlike her usual interactions with other people—she had been tempted to flag her down and apologize. Instead, she had stubbornly refused to do more than glance Casey's way.

As soon as the car doors shut again, the resident dogs that were already in the kennels sensed the newcomers' arrival and started barking in a chaotic chorus, and Iris lurched forward as the shepherd tried to drag her toward the other animals. She didn't want to terrify the cat by taking her into the dogs' area, so she held her ground until Leo, Agatha's husband, came and took the crate from her.

"Thanks," she said, relieved to have help. "She can go in Christine's bungalow for now. She's pregnant, so she needs more peace and quiet than she'd get in the cat rooms."

Once Leo had taken the cat toward the little house closest to Iris's, she took the shepherd to the main kennels. She knew she could trust Leo to get the mama cat settled with a bed, food, and water. When Iris bought the shelter, Agatha and Leo were already living on the property and working with the animals. Iris had been reluctant to have a ready-made staff, preferring instead to have a choice in the people she hired, but she hadn't had the nerve to make the retired couple leave the place they had made into their home. After about a week, she was ready to beg them to stay if they ever tried to leave her. They worked tirelessly and selflessly to help every dog and cat that came through the shelter, and they had taken Iris under their wings as well. Christine, the summer intern, had recently gone back to school, leaving the three of them to handle work that was tiring on a good day and backbreaking after an event like the quake.

Iris walked the dog down the main aisle, bordered on each side by large chain-link kennels. The barking seemed loud from the parking area, and once she was right in the midst of it, the noise battered her without any buffering walls or distance. Iris liked the sound—luckily—and she was able to pick out every individual dog's voice, but the sheer number of animals made her shoulder muscles tighten with stress. They were always overflowing with miscellaneous pets in need of homes, even in this small community of islands, and they had added nearly a quarter again of their current population since yesterday. She felt like a turtle trying to pull its head into the safety of its shell, and she made a conscious effort to relax her shoulders and stretch her neck a little taller. She might feel like curling in a ball and hiding from the shaken world, but she could at least look like she didn't.

A double-sized kennel in front of the office served as a holding area for recent arrivals, and Iris put the shepherd inside it with the two smaller dogs since the three had gotten along okay in close quarters during the trip here from Lopez. Iris walked into the office and flipped on the light switch automatically before remembering that the electricity had been out since the day before. She was surprised to see the lights come on.

"Oh," she said. It was such a small sound, but the relief and gratitude it contained made her feel close to tears. "The power is back."

"They started working on clearing the lines on our street just after you left this morning," Agatha said. "I thought it would be a nice welcome-home present for you."

"One of the best I could have imagined," Iris said. She dropped into her desk chair and felt her shoulders curl forward again. No electricity had meant no water because they were on a well. They had a powerful generator—a necessity out here where the ocean-borne storms could do serious damage—but the beast guzzled fuel faster than Iris could keep it filled, sucking up money that was needed for the animals. Iris appreciated having the machine when she needed it, but she was always happy to turn it off again.

"We had an owner show up," Agatha continued. She lifted a fat calico off a pile of papers and relocated her to another part of the desk. The cat—aptly named Lazy Susan—barely opened her eyes long enough to give Agatha an indignant glare before falling asleep again. "Those two shih tzus you found near the post office got loose when a tree fell across her fence."

Iris sighed. Wonderful. Two dogs out and three in. The equation didn't balance, but it was better than she had expected. Agatha shook her head.

"Don't get too excited. One of the workers from the power company found a stray in the woods a few blocks from here. Some kind of hound mix. Looked like he had crawled through a swamp to get here, but underneath all the muck he's healthy and has a nice coat. Belongs to someone."

Agatha continued to gather papers and put them in front of Iris. She was as efficient as always, despite the earthquake and its frenetic aftermath. At first glance, Iris had thought Agatha looked like the grandmotherly, bridge-playing, cookie-baking type, but she had been mistaken. Agatha had spent decades running a wholesale nursery, and she did most of the maintenance at the shelter. Just last night, she had been wielding a chainsaw and hacking through some of the debris from fallen trees. Iris had tried to stop her and do the manual labor on her own, but Agatha had been relentless, as usual. Still, even with the two of them working, they had managed to clear only a small section of the property.

Iris filled out the four intake forms Agatha gave her while she cringed inside at the thought of all the work still in front of them. The shelter's three acres were thick with fir trees, making it secluded and peaceful most of the time, and a big mess after the tremors had tossed every loose branch and needle to the ground. A few of the trees had fallen, blocking walking trails and destroying one of the exercise pens.

Iris signed the last form with a flourish, out-processing the shih tzus. Most of the new arrivals would have owners who had lost them during the confusion of the quake and were looking for them. She would do whatever it took to reunite them.

"We can leave the three Lopez dogs where they are for now," Iris said, mentally touring the kennels. "Since Jack and Gus will be in the infirmary for a few days, I can get their runs repaired and then we can move the three out of the intake pen. Oh, wait. Sasha hates little dogs, so the Chihuahuas can't go there. Maybe if we move Jupiter…"

Iris unpinned the kennel schematic from the wall behind her desk and she and Agatha erased and penciled in names until they were accommodating every dog's needs and preferences. As soon as another animal came to the shelter, they'd have to go through the same process yet again.

Agatha went outside to help Leo move the dogs while Iris got her tote box of tools and headed out to the damaged runs. She stopped by the small infirmary to see the two dogs that had been injured yesterday when trees had crashed down on their runs. The room was basic, but filled their needs for most of the routine injuries and illnesses they encountered. For more serious problems, the animals would stay with the vet. A large shelf held various first aid supplies, and a fridge full of vaccines and puppy formula stood next to it. A simple metal table was in the center of the room, and the far wall was lined with four narrow indoor pens.

She went into the first one and knelt next to the black-and-white freckled dog that was lying on a round corduroy bed. He gently licked her hand as she peeled back his bandage and checked the gash on his leg. A neat row of stitches—courtesy of Iris's friend and vet, Bianca, who had taken time out of her harried night and made a house call—stretched from Gus's shoulder nearly to his paw. She stuck the bandage back in place and scratched behind his ears with suddenly shaky hands.

As long as she was taking care of the animals, she could keep her mind off the earthquake and the fear it had shaken loose inside her. Once she stopped, even for a moment, it rippled through her again.

Iris sat cross-legged in the pen, one hand stroking Gus and the other reaching into the adjoining run to tickle Jack's chin. He had three paws wrapped in white gauze because he had gotten out of his damaged kennel and trotted through the shards of glass from the shattered office window. She was lucky that these were the worst of the injuries. The cats had looked like an electric charge had run through their small house, making their backs arch and their tails fluff to twice the normal size, but after an hour or so, they had gone back to their usual unruffled state. The dogs had barked and howled through the night, but they were settled by morning. Aside from a few bandages and piles of broken branches, the exterior signs of the disaster were abating. Inside, though, Iris still felt aftershocks, as if she had a fault line of her own running through her body.

Casey had made her internal faults shift again, until they scraped against each other and made her erupt with anger. She hadn't been mad at Casey, and she really had no reason to blame her for being interested in studying the earthquake. Casey had looked cool and in control. Untouched by the disaster that had frightened Iris to the core. She hadn't seemed to have family she was worried about or broken belongings she was mourning. Iris was a little jealous of Casey's apparently unencumbered state. She also was a whole lot tired of being afraid all the time. Even if she had been in Casey's position, without a care in the world besides her search for knowledge, the earthquake would still have reduced Iris to a quivering mass of fear.

She got to her feet and gave both dogs a treat before heading back to Jack's normal kennel, at the end of the shed row. She put on a pair of heavy work gloves, about two sizes too big for her slender hands, and grabbed hold of the heavy limb that had landed across the back corner. She tugged and pushed, trying to rock the branch loose, as dislodged bark dusted her face and her hands scratched for traction in the loose gloves. She paused for a moment, leaning against a wooden post to catch her breath while feisty Sasha barked and spun in circles in the kennel next door.

Damn. She had been miserable enough having lingering fear from the quake reassert itself in her rare idle moments, but now every time she stopped what she was doing, Casey managed to insinuate herself into Iris's thoughts as well. Iris could fill most of her time with work, with talking to Agatha and Leo, with caring for the dogs and cats, but she had to rest occasionally. Would Casey infiltrate every spare moment?

Iris pulled off one of her gloves and wiped a few bits of flaked bark out of her eyes. Her response to Casey on the ferry only managed to emphasize how out of control Iris was feeling right now. Casey was unfazed by the earthquake, practically elated by the opportunity to study it, while Iris was overwhelmed and trembling. Casey was independent while Iris was bound to her shelter.

Iris put on her glove and reached for the branch again. She braced her foot against the post for leverage and pulled hard, finally wresting the limb free of its wedged position. She fell backward and landed on her ass with the branch on top of her. Very undignified, but Sasha seemed happy to have her at ground level.

Iris shoved the limb aside and lay back, resting until her breathing was back to normal. She stood up and got a pair of fence pliers and some loose pieces of heavy-gauge wire out of her toolbox. She was struggling to straighten the crumpled chain link when Leo appeared by her side and reached for the jagged edge that had been severed by the thick branch.

"Thanks," she gasped, using her weight to pull the other side of the torn fence to meet the part he held. She worked one hand loose from the fence and the too-large glove and joined the two edges together with a length of spare wire.

"Careful, there are some sharp ends up here," he said as Iris added another wire, slowly suturing the gashed fence with strands of metal.

"I've got it. Just one more, and...Ouch!" Iris raked her finger across the ragged edge and drew blood. She grimaced at the throbbing pain and tried to hold the finger out of the way as she twisted the wires tightly with the pliers. She cut the loose ends and tamped them down so none of the dogs would be in danger from the patchwork job.

"Told you," Leo said with a teasing smile as he took a hand-kerchief out of his pocket and wrapped Iris's bleeding finger. He sighed and gave her hand a gentle pat. "You and Agatha are working too hard. I wish I—"

"Don't, Leo. Please." His chronic back problems had been part of the reason he and Agatha had sold their Seattle nursery and come to the islands to retire. "You do more than your share in the kennels and with the animals. You know I couldn't run this place without you."

He shook his head, but let the subject drop. "I put a box and some blankets in one of the bungalow's closets, and your mama cat seems to be happy there. I'd say she'll have her litter soon, maybe a few days. I just hope the stress of yesterday didn't do any serious harm."

Iris frowned. "Me, too. I'm headed back to the house to shower, and I'll give Bianca a call. See if she can stop by and check on the cat since I don't want to pack her in that crate and move her again. Are you and Agatha coming by for dinner?"

"Yes. We wouldn't miss one of your home-cooked meals."

"Home-thawed is more like it," Iris said. She left Leo to sweep the dust and debris out of the newly repaired kennel while she put the tools away and walked to her small house. She stopped by the bungalow on the way, and found the pregnant gray cat hiding under the bed and glaring at her with angry green eyes. Iris checked to make sure she had enough food and water, and then went home.

As soon as she got to the flagstone path leading to her door, she could smell the herbs Agatha had planted in her front garden. Some of them had already flowered and gone to seed, past their growing season, but some, like the piney rosemary and fragrant lemon balm, were still growing strong. Iris plucked a few leaves of oregano as she walked past. She would add them to the lasagna she had taken out of the freezer to thaw this morning, layering a note of freshness into the pre-made meal.

Another difference between her and someone like Casey, Iris thought with a humorless laugh. Would Casey make a bunch of meals and freeze them just in case? Iris doubted it. It wasn't as if Iris had prophesied the earthquake somehow. She just *always* had food on hand in case something went wrong and she wasn't able to cook. But Casey didn't seem to be a worrier.

Iris opened her door and went into the house, feeling some of her stress ease away. She had cleaned last night, frantically sweeping up broken knickknacks and tossing damaged furniture into the garage. She had wiped everything that remained with vanilla-scented wood polish while the windows had stood open to let the fresh—and very chilly—air inside. Soon she'd add the aroma of baking tomato sauce and cheese to the comforting scent of home.

Iris got in the shower and washed the messiness of the day away with steaming hot water. Of course, Casey followed her into the shower, too. Iris scrunched her eyes shut and tried to ignore the image of a naked Casey lounging casually against the tiled wall. She'd surely be as self-assured and laid-back without clothes as she was while wearing them. Iris leaned her forehead against the tile, close to the spot where she imagined Casey's shoulder rested, and let the water pulse against her shoulders and back. Casey had been a disconcerting part of a difficult day, but right now, for one unguarded moment, Iris let herself feel a little comfort from their imagined closeness.

Chapter Five

Casey eased into a sitting position in the cab of her truck. Her head felt permanently tilted to the right after spending the night wedged against the driver's side door, and she awkwardly massaged her muscles with one hand until she could lift her chin again. She was surprised she ached so much since she had spent most of the night wide awake, staring at the readouts from the seismometers she had deployed along the desolate stretch of road where her truck was now parked.

A series of tremors—most too gentle to be detected by humans—had rocked the island while Casey watched the readings splash across her monitor. She had noticed two of the higher magnitude events, but she wasn't sure if it was because she saw the evidence of them and imagined she felt the movement to match, or if she had actually felt the ground move. She wasn't the type to stick her head in the sand and ignore geologic inevitabilities, and she wasn't about to pretend that earthquakes weren't a real danger in the Northwest, but she had longed for a few hours of peace and ignorance last night.

Had Iris felt the aftershocks? Casey wouldn't have been surprised to hear that Iris's dogs and cats had been extra jumpy, since evidence suggested that animals were much more sensitive to seismic activity than humans. Casey pictured Iris as she looked yesterday, with frown lines etched in her forehead and exhaustion evident in the dark circles under her lovely eyes with those incredible lashes. She didn't like to think of her having even more to worry about, although the chance of another high magnitude seismic event wasn't out of the question given the amount of activity Casey had been observing.

She got out of the truck and bent forward, stretching her tight lower back muscles. She had spent an inordinate amount of time thinking about Iris while she was scrunched in the driver's seat, hoping no one would come by and arrest her for vagrancy. At first, her thoughts had been similar to yesterday's, as she alternated between memories of their argument and memories of the way the corners of Iris's eyes crinkled endearingly when she had briefly laughed about the crowd on the ferry.

She hadn't been laughing when she berated Casey for having a job, though.

Casey sighed and rubbed her hand across her face. She didn't need to go in those circles again. She had followed her spiraling thoughts for hours in the dark cab, caught between wanting to yell at Iris and wanting to hunt her down and sleep with her. Admittedly, the latter option sounded more and more appealing as the hours wore on, partly because she figured Iris had an actual bed. A comfortable, soft, sheet-covered bed.

Casey got back in her truck with a groan and started the engine. Luckily, the temperatures had been cool but not anywhere near freezing, or she would have needed to keep the engine running the whole night. Instead, she had gotten away with wearing most of the clothes she had in her bag. She turned the heater on full blast and pulled onto Westside Road, passing the state park at Lime Kiln Point and continuing along the coast for another mile until she came to an overgrown dirt road. One of her array of small seismometers had stopped transmitting just before dawn, shortly after a sudden gust of wind had buffeted the truck and yanked Casey out of sleep. She figured a fallen branch or a curious raccoon had toppled the instrument. The protective case should have prevented any serious damage, but Casey wanted to get the machine working again as soon as possible.

She parked behind a screen of trees and walked deeper into the woods, batting at massive spiderwebs that must have been spun overnight. She shuddered at the creepy feeling of delicate and unseen threads touching her hands and face, and she tried to pretend that the webs were empty and there were no huge spiders attached to them. She was glad no one was around to see her as she whacked at every tickle on her skin as if a hairy tarantula was migrating up her arm. The logical side of her brain told her she was in more danger of picking up a tick and getting Lyme disease than dying of a spider bite, but the nonlogical side—usually the side that kept to itself and made only rare appearances—wasn't reassured by that information.

She wished Iris could see her right now, risking her life, sort of, to collect data that would be used to help scientists learn how to predict earthquakes with precision someday. Maybe she wouldn't be so quick to judge Casey's level of compassion if she understood what she was trying to do out here.

What did she care what Iris thought of her?

Casey realized she'd asked herself the same question with varying levels of righteous indignation at least a hundred times since yesterday's ferry ride. She asked the question, but she didn't want to look too closely at the answer. Iris had gotten to her somehow, and that was enough to make Casey realize she was best avoided.

She pushed Iris out of her mind and walked on, finally coming to a curved clearing. She gave one last exaggerated spider-removing shudder before walking over clumps of dry brown grass and toward the water. The grassy area ended with a three-foot drop to a thin strip of rocky shoreline, but Casey stayed on top of the little bluff and looked out at the slate-gray water. Ahead of her was Haro Strait and the dark silhouette of Vancouver Island, Canada. To her left was the Strait of Juan de Fuca and—too far to see in the murky weather—the Olympic Peninsula of Washington State. Casey stood quietly for a few moments, marveling at the feeling of being totally isolated in between the two massive countries.

She raised onto her toes and squinted toward the horizon when she saw half a dozen tall black fins cutting through the waves on the Washington side of the strait. If she'd had a chance to get back to her apartment before this unscheduled trip, she would have brought binoculars with her, but she was terribly unprepared for even a week on this remote island, far from the glorious benefits of civilization, like functioning hotels. She stared into the distance until the fins disappeared from sight, and then she turned inland again with a sigh.

She traipsed across the meadow, counting trees as she went, and ducked under a bush with sparse foliage. She found her seismometer where she had left it, but askew, and she pulled it out of its hiding place. She looked around for a place to sit, but had to opt for the ground. What the hell, she was a mess anyway. She pried open the case and used a pair of slim needle-nose pliers to reattach a wire that had come loose.

She'd hid the instruments carefully, but the field machines weren't exactly top of the line. The UW lab had massive and highly sensitive instruments in place around the Northwest—all protected much better than her portable machine was by the bush she had chosen. Sometimes, though, having someone in the field getting detailed readings from selected areas using intuition and observation provided more information than the fancier equipment.

Casey finished making her adjustments and was about to replace the canister, but she decided to move the instrument to a different location based on the trends she had seen in her readings the night before. She tucked it under her arm and hiked back to the truck, trying to retrace her steps exactly so she'd be traveling through a web-free zone. She got off course somehow though, and ended up wading through a thick layer of bracken ferns. The coarse, lacy fronds brushed against her as she walked, parting as her legs pushed through them and slapping back into place in her wake. She held her free arm down by her side, her fingers outstretched, and let the leaves brush against her hands.

She had been in cities for a long time, from Chicago to Palo Alto to Seattle. She belonged in them, amid the bustle of urban life, but she was surprised to discover that something about this island was affecting her deep inside. Her nerve endings seemed more alive, more aware. Every touch, whether it was the rasp of tree bark or the ghostly tingle of an ocean breeze coming off the Sound, seemed to wake her up, out of some sort of dream, a little bit at a time.

She pushed through the last of the ferns and emerged from the woods a short distance past her truck. She walked back to it and put the seismometer on the passenger seat before driving to the new location. She supposed she was just feeling what hikers and outdoorsy types always droned on about—some sort of communion with Mother Nature. *She* would attribute it to a lot of months without a vacation that culminated in a trip to Stanford, Land of the Exes. She just needed a break, something completely different from her normal life, and the ocean and trees were doing the trick.

Casey wouldn't have minded a little more communion with Iris, too, if they hadn't been so at odds with each other on the ferry. She lumped her strange obsession with the near-stranger in with her unexpected enjoyment of nature. Iris, with her fierce devotion to her animals and to her community, was unlike anyone else Casey knew. She was a change of pace, that was all.

Casey could learn from this and solve her fixation with logic. She didn't need to move to the middle of nowhere and live like Thoreau, and she certainly didn't need to track down Iris and ask her to stop criticizing Casey long enough to go on a date with her. What she needed was to do her job, return to Seattle, and take up a hobby or something to get her out of her rut. Skydiving? Rock climbing? They had indoor versions that didn't involve actual rocks, didn't they?

She couldn't find another offshoot road leading to the spot where she wanted to place the seismometer, so she parked along the side of the road and started another trailblazing hike through the woods. She heard a dog barking in the distance, reminding her of Iris yet again. Was Iris really that different from her after all? Casey cared about her world and the people in it just as much as Iris did, she was sure. She just had a different way of expressing her concern. A way that Iris had been unable to see. The animal-loving thing wasn't a comparison Casey could make, either. It wasn't like Iris liked animals and Casey didn't. She just wasn't familiar with them. Or comfortable around them. They were messy and unpredictable. Two things Casey was *not*.

Casey paused to get her bearings. Where was the water? Which way led back to her truck? She hoped she'd be able to find her way back by nightfall. She had complained about using the cramped truck cab as a bed, but it beat sleeping on the fir needle covered ground.

As she stood quietly, she caught another whiff of smoke in the air. Yesterday when she had explored the tiny island, she had seen several small, intentional fires lit by people who must have been clearing away the debris left over from the earthquake. The smell was out of place and slightly disconcerting when she was in the middle of the flammable woods. Casey veered in the direction she thought led to the shoreline.

The dog's bark sounded closer, each woof ending with a drawn-out howled note. This area was isolated, but not deserted, and she had passed several houses and farms on her way here from her last stop. The animal must be guarding one of those homes.

Casey shifted the seismometer in her arms. It was getting heavy, and she was getting tired from lack of sleep and the unaccustomed traipsing through the forest. She fished a strip of pink plastic out of her pocket and tied it on a tree. She walked a few yards away because she wanted the marker to lead her to the general area where she had placed the instrument, and not to give the exact location away to anyone who happened by.

After securing the seismometer under a thick berry bush and earning several scrapes in the process, she stood silently and listened to the dog. She should turn around and get back to the truck. Go into town and see if Jazz was making something good for lunch. Do another round of hotel visits, hoping to find one that was open for business.

Instead, she continued the way she had been going, following the baying sound. She would just make sure there was a house up ahead, where the vocal animal was probably waiting to bite any intruders who ventured onto its property.

After ten more minutes of walking through brush that was determined to either scratch her or snag her clothing, Casey began to doubt herself. She wasn't seeing any sign of a residence near here. No paths or clearings or sounds other than the dog and the occasional chirp or flutter of a bird. She felt her chest tighten every time the dog howled, and the sound seemed more plaintive and urgent to her as she got closer. She batted a thin hazelnut tree out of her way and nearly stepped on the dog.

She stopped where she was and watched the animal. He—or she?—was a medium-sized reddish brown dog. Its coat was matted, with streaks of mud across its shoulder and twigs trailing from its tail. It strained toward her, but something seemed to be holding it in place. Casey inched closer and saw the frayed remnant of a fishing net wrapped around the exposed roots of a tree and the dog's back legs.

Casey's experience with dogs might be limited, but she was pretty sure that any trapped animal would be likely to snap at someone who got too close. What if she hurt it when she tried to untangle the net? It'd probably take a piece of her arm in exchange.

She sighed. Of course she couldn't leave it here. She'd have to take her chances.

The dog whined and wagged its tail as she stepped toward it. She tentatively took hold of the net where it was snagged on the roots and tugged. Nothing. She pulled harder, but the fibers wouldn't give. She'd have to remove it from the dog instead.

"Hey, fella. Or girl. Whatever you are. Don't mind me, but I'm going to lift your paw."

The dog whined again and nudged her hand. For the second time in two days, she had the cold nose of a dog touch her skin. She lived in the heart of the city, in an apartment that didn't allow pets, and she couldn't remember the last time she had been around animals. The dog's winter coat felt thick and wooly against her fingers as she carefully unwound the tightly twisted net, and more of those ambiguous childhood memories came to her. She was somewhere with her mother. A petting zoo? Where would they have found a petting zoo? She couldn't place the scene, but she remembered snatches of tactile sensations. The tickling lips of a miniature horse as it took a treat from her open palm. The variations in fur, from coarse to liquid soft, of the different animals. Smells of hay and wood chips and animals.

Casey refocused on the present and the dog in front of her. She knelt next to it and felt it lean against her while she worked. Far from biting or growling at her, it huddled closer, as if aware that she was trying to help. The stubbornly knotted nylon took enough of her concentration to keep more memories from rising to the surface of her mind. She habitually kept herself far removed from her early childhood memories, but she didn't realize just how much distance she maintained until she was faced with one of these unexpected triggers.

The last section of the net finally came loose, and Casey and the now-free dog stared at each other.

"So, um, I've got to get going," Casey said. She couldn't bring herself to do the baby talk thing with an animal, so she talked to it as if addressing an adult human. Still, she felt weirdly shy talking to a dog at all, unlike the ease she usually felt around people.

What was she supposed to do now? Force the dog to go with her? Leave it alone in the woods? She tried to give it an option, even though she knew it didn't understand her. "I guess you live around here somewhere and you probably want to get back home, but if you don't, you can come with me."

Casey got to her feet and started walking away. She was relieved that the dog followed her—in fact, she had been hoping it would instead of bolting away—but she wasn't sure what to do with it now. She wasn't going to be on the islands long, and even if she temporarily lost her mind and wanted to keep the dog, her apartment wouldn't allow her to have a hamster, let alone this big, slobbery creature.

The animal probably had a home near here, anyway. It was a little skinnier than she thought it should be, but not terribly unhealthy looking, and its nails and paws didn't give her the impression that it had been running loose for long. It needed a bath, but then she did, too, so she couldn't pass judgment. The dog stuck close to her heels until they got within sight of the truck, and then it ran ahead of her and stood by the passenger door.

She opened the door and the dog vaulted into the truck. A boy dog. Okay. Casey shut the door, careful not to slam it on the feathery, wagging tail, and then she got in as well. She'd stop by some of the houses she had passed on her way here and ask about him. Surely the dog belonged to one of the places nearby, or someone would at least recognize him and point her in the direction of his home. Then she'd go back to Friday Harbor and look for her own place to stay, even though she doubted any of the hotels had magically reopened overnight. Worst case, if both plans failed, she'd sleep in the truck once more. At least this time, she'd have a furry, warm pillow.

Chapter Six

Iris wrinkled her nose as she opened another can of dog food and dumped the contents into a stainless-steel bowl. She looked at the picture on the label, showing a pot roast meal that looked fit to serve at a dinner party, and then at the brown glob in the bowl. She usually fed dry food, but the dogs who needed to gain weight or who were finicky eaters got this glorious slop. Luckily the dogs weren't pretentious gourmands, and they loved this stuff.

She carried two bowls of food into the infirmary and gave them to Gus and Jack. They started eating immediately, with vigorously waving tails, while she went outside to fill water buckets. She came around the corner of the shed row with the hose crimped in her hand and nearly ran into Casey.

Casey. At her shelter. With a dog.

Water dripped from the nozzle as Iris stood in silence. She had thought of Casey altogether too often since they met two days ago, and she wondered for a brief moment if this was really her, or if she was just imagining her again.

"Hi," said Casey.

Yes, she was real. The golden retriever sat close against her leg, with his tongue lolling to one side. The reddish tones in his hair matched Casey's, and they both looked like they had been charging through the woods for a few days.

"Hi," Iris answered. She felt a silly grin stretch across her face—she hadn't used her smiling muscles much lately, and her control over them felt rusty. She cleared her throat and tried to relax her expression so it looked less giddy.

"I found a dog," Casey continued, gesturing unnecessarily at the one sitting at her feet. Iris stared at Casey's hand as it waved in the direction of the retriever. She remembered Casey's expressive use of her hands as she had chattered on about what she considered to be the fascinating aspects of fault lines and earthquakes during their ferry ride. She also remembered how she had reacted to Casey's words.

"I see that. He's a handsome boy, so I'm sure you'll be very happy with him." Iris knew she was intentionally misunderstanding Casey's meaning, but she wasn't sure why. She normally prided herself on being a nice person, apologizing if she was inadvertently rude and not going out of her way to make people uncomfortable, but Casey brought out something else in her. Something mean? No. Something intense and scary, and it made Iris want to push her away.

"No, he's not mine. He's a stray, and a friend of mine from Friday Harbor told me to bring him here."

Had Casey already made a friend in town, or was this someone she already knew? Iris wouldn't have been surprised at the former, since Casey seemed to have an easy way of talking with strangers. Iris had noticed her relaxed way of striking up a conversation when they had first met. She had been envious of it, and that might have contributed to her cranky mood because it seemed to point out a flaw in Iris herself by comparison.

"We're pretty full right now," Iris said. She stepped closer and crouched down to the dog's level, reaching out with her left hand and letting him sniff her. She inhaled, too, getting a good whiff of a dog that had been rolling in God-knew-what as well as a hint of Casey in the background. She smelled delicious—literally. Like she had just been cooking with exotic spices. A hint of cumin and a heavier layer of cardamom. Yum.

She accidentally loosened her hold on the folded hose and a spray of water shot across the aisle, making Casey and the dog back up and out of the way. Iris tightened her grip again and stood, stepping away from the pair. She needed to do whatever it took to move Casey along.

"Of course, we'll take him. Let me put the hose away, and I'll get an intake form for you to sign."

Casey just nodded, watching her with an inscrutable expression. Was she about to laugh? Iris wasn't sure, but she was tired of feeling out of control when Casey was near her. Irrationally angry one minute, and a bumbling fool the next.

She dragged the hose back to the spigot and turned off the water. She took her time rolling the hose into a tidy coil even though she'd be back to watering the animals as soon as she shooed Casey on her way. She needed the extra seconds, though, to get herself back to her usual even-tempered self. Get a grip.

As she approached Casey again, she decided to bring up their ferry argument. She'd laugh off her overreaction and prove to Casey—and to herself—that she was composed and steady. Her steps faltered as she realized she had spent most of her life wishing she *wasn't* that way. She'd finally found someone who pushed her out of her comfort zone, and all she wanted was to go back to normal. Iris wasn't prepared for quite as much stimulation as Casey seemed to provoke in her, although she had been coping with it just fine when she was alone last night and imagining Casey with her, touching her, pulling her out of normal and into something so much more…

Why did her mind have to go there? Iris took a deep breath, held it for a few seconds, and then exhaled. "I have the paper-work in the office," she said, leading the way. Casey followed with the dog at her side, but she paused before she entered the room.

"Is it okay if he's in here, or should he wait outside?"

Iris thought she was joking at first. There were dog beds near the desk, and the fat cat was asleep on top of it. Crates of pet food were stacked against the far wall, and Iris had tripped over a chew toy on her way across the room. If this place didn't look pet friendly, Iris didn't know what would. But Casey stood in the doorway, barring the retriever's entrance, and her expression didn't have a hint of humor in it.

"It's a shelter, Casey," she said. "The animals belong everywhere. Come in, both of you."

Casey stepped inside, and the dog trotted past her and made a beeline for the calico. He rested his chin on the edge of the desk and stared at the cat. She barely bothered to open her eyes, but her purring increased in volume and the dog whined in response.

Iris had been ready to scoop Lazy Susan into her arms at the slightest hint of aggression, although the cat had been known to show surprising swiftness when she needed to put a too-assertive dog in its place, but the retriever's posture and movements were nonthreatening. Iris reached across the desk and rubbed his soft ears.

"He's a sweet boy," she said, going to the file cabinet and pulling out an intake form. "I'm sure his owners will turn up eventually." She cleared her throat and continued, in a voice so studiously casual it didn't sound like it belonged to her. "Hey, before we get to this, I wanted to apologize for the ferry ride. I shouldn't have snapped at you just because you came here to do your job. It's really none of my business whether you care about the people on the islands or not. Now, if you can just fill out this top section and sign here."

Casey ignored Iris's instructions. "But I do care."

"All right. I'm just saying it doesn't matter if you do or—"

"I *do*."

"All right," Iris repeated in an emphatic voice. "I meant I shouldn't have gotten angry, even if you don't—"

"But I do."

Iris glared at Casey, who glared back. The retriever still had his chin on the desk, but his eyes moved back and forth between the two of them. Even Lazy Susan had woken up and was watching their middle-school drama—not that Iris had ever been this testy, even during her preteen and teen years. So much for composure. Iris decided her original plan to get Casey out of here as soon as possible was the best choice. She turned Iris inside out.

"You care. I got it," Iris said. She was tempted to add the phrase *but even if you didn't* because once she stopped focusing on her own disconcerting inability to remain calm, she could see that she was making Casey just as crazy as she felt in Casey's presence. She managed to keep from voicing the childish retort, though. "Will you sign this form? Then I can take the dog from you."

"Somebody needs a bath."

Iris dropped the pen and cracked her shin against the desk at the sudden sound of Leo's voice. Casey stepped backward with a startled expression, tripping over a dog toy in the shape of a rolled-up newspaper. It squeaked loudly, and the retriever pounced on it.

"Oh, sorry. I slept in my truck last night…"

"He certainly does, Leo," Iris said at the same time. Then, turning to Casey, "What?"

"Nothing." Casey tried to get the toy from her dog, but he thought she was playing a game and he wouldn't let go.

Leo went over and slipped a collar around the dog's neck, leading him through the office door. Leo tilted his head as if asking a question when he walked past Iris, and she shook her head slightly in response. She knew he must be thinking about the empty bungalow not more than two hundred feet from where they stood. Of course, it wasn't completely empty. Still, there were two bedrooms, and the pregnant gray cat really didn't need them both.

"You slept in your truck?" Iris asked once Leo and the dog had left. Casey seemed a little forlorn without the retriever by her side, but Iris was probably imagining it. Even though Casey had caught the shepherd for her on the ferry and had rescued this dog, she didn't seem natural around the animals. Indifferent, maybe?

"The hotels are closed." Casey shrugged. "No big deal. The cab is pretty comfortable."

Yeah, right. "I warned you about that on the ferry."

"Like I said, it doesn't matter. I'm here for a couple of days. A week or two tops. I'm sure businesses will be opening again soon."

Casey walked over to the desk and picked up the pen. She signed the form and slid it across the desk toward Iris. "Thanks for giving him a place to stay."

Casey seemed awkward somehow, but Iris wasn't sure why. She had figured *she* was the one who was discombobulated by Casey, but she was seeing signs that the effect might work both ways.

"It's my job," Iris said. She heard the echo of Casey's statement on the ferry in her words and she couldn't resist adding to it. "I care about the animals."

"All right," Casey said, mimicking Iris's previous staccato tone exactly, "but even if you didn't..."

Iris laughed out loud, and her unexpected response to Casey's playfulness was as disconcerting to her as her earlier annoyance. The only two times she had honestly laughed and felt the corresponding release of tension since the earthquake had been when she was talking to Casey. Unfortunately, Casey caused her share of tension as well. Still, the shared joke was more effective than Iris's apology had been. Even if it hadn't been, she had no real choice except to offer her the use of the bungalow. She didn't know how she'd manage to have Casey nearby even for a week or less, but she'd have to do her best. It would be too unkind to make her sleep in a truck when Iris had a perfectly good room available. Only a short walk from Iris's own bedroom...

She hesitated a moment while her daydreaming mind whipped up a quick fantasy about a midnight visit to Casey's bed, and Casey spoke before Iris.

"I know you're packed with animals right now, so I can pay you for his food or board, or whatever you need," she said.

"Or I can make it up to you by helping around here when I'm not working. I noticed some damage to the kennels and all the fallen branches. I'd be glad to help out. I have plenty of free time and nothing at all to fill it."

Casey could obviously see that Iris was desperate for help, but she looked as though she needed Iris, too, to say yes and give her something to do. Was she a workaholic? Unable to relax without constant activity? Or was she trying to escape from something besides boredom?

Whatever the reason, Iris needed her. She and Agatha would never find enough hours to get everything done.

"That'd be great, if you're serious about the offer. And I can repay you for the work by letting you stay here at the shelter."

"In a kennel?" Casey gave her a lopsided, adorably self-deprecating smile. "Not that I'm complaining after sleeping crammed against the truck door last night. Hell, a few minutes ago I was wondering if I'd be able to sneak one of these dog beds out without you noticing. I was going to put it in the bed of the truck."

"I think the human bed in the bungalow might be more comfortable, and smell better, too." Iris didn't mention that her own bed was even nicer than the one in the interns' cottage. She cleared her throat. Her fantasies were fine when she was alone at night, but she needed to keep them at bay while she was around Casey. "Do you want to keep the dog with you? Leo will have him cleaned up in no time."

"You mean keep him in the house? Not here in the kennel?"

Casey looked...what? Confused? Hopeful? Iris dismissed the latter idea. It was too absurd. If she had wanted the dog with her, she would have just asked, wouldn't she?

"Yes, in the house. The interns always have one or two with them. They're great company, and the personal interaction is healthy for the animals."

"Sure, I guess that would be fine. I'll get my things."

Casey turned away abruptly, and Iris jumped into action just as quickly. The retriever seemed well-behaved around cats, but Iris would put up some baby gates to give the cat a safe place to get away. She'd also grab a couple of her frozen meals and put them in the bungalow's fridge. This was why she'd made them in the first place. For unexpected situations.

Unexpected. Unsettling.

And far too exhilarating.

CHAPTER SEVEN

Casey carried her small bag to the bungalow as she struggled to sort out her mixed feelings about staying on Iris's property. Iris affected her too much. Usually Casey was in control, but around Iris she felt buffeted by their conversations, swinging from irritation to laughter much too quickly for comfort. Iris didn't understand Casey's job or her personal investment in it. She was tied to this tiny island and to her kennel full of animals. What could they possibly have in common, besides the physical attraction Casey felt every time they were near each other?

But Casey didn't have many options. She couldn't keep the dog with her, and she wasn't going to abandon him after going from house to house near where she'd found him without anyone recognizing him. What else was she supposed to do?

She shifted the strap of her bag higher on her shoulder as she turned off the gravel walkway and onto a path made of gray octagon and square pavers. She stepped carefully from octagon to octagon, admiring the neat, symmetrical pattern and trying to conveniently forget her earlier visit to Jazz's restaurant, where she had annihilated a huge plate of homemade fries smothered in curry sauce while the dog chewed happily on a bone at her feet. She had asked Jazz to recommend a place to take the dog, fully expecting her to offer Iris's name, but Jazz had instead told her to contact the San Juan County Humane Society on Orcas Island. Casey had tried to be subtle about soliciting a different suggestion, but eventually she had come right out and asked for Iris by name. Jazz had paused, giving her an annoyingly knowing grin, before she wrote Iris's address down on a piece of paper. *I'm pretty sure her shelter is full right now, but maybe she'll make an exception for you. I mean...for your dog.*

Casey knocked on the door of the little house. It didn't matter how she got here. Iris needed help cleaning up after the earthquake, and she needed a place to stay. End of story.

Iris opened the door and smiled at her, and Casey started editing that story in her head. Did it have to end so soon? Unfortunately, it had too many what-ifs in it. *What if* Casey didn't live in Seattle, miles away in terms of distance and atmosphere? *What if* Iris wasn't tied to this shelter?

Casey didn't need another reminder of the pain caused by ill-advised dating choices, and she wasn't about to add a potential third ex to the mix. She and Sophie had differences that complemented each other. Then she had picked Shelby because they were similar. After those two fiascos, finishing grad school single seemed the prudent choice, and then she'd crack the dating code and start again. But grad school segued into her first job, and as soon as she had gotten comfortable there, she had received the offer from the UW lab. More upheaval, more excuses to avoid the dating pool.

She still hadn't figured out the formula for selecting the right person to date, and until she did, she wasn't going to take a chance that a random encounter with a beautiful woman meant they were destined to be together.

Iris's smile made it oh, so difficult to listen to common sense. Casey had heard the phrase *a smile that lights up a room* plenty of times, but she had never fully comprehended it until now. Iris made the world brighter somehow, with a warm and earthy glow that reminded Casey of burnished wood and the heavenly scent of vanilla and kitchen-y spices.

Casey had to face the fact that she had come here on purpose, like a child daring herself to find out how long she could stand holding her fingers on the hot surface of a stovetop. Iris made her feel as if she was burning up, but she relished the sensation even though she knew she should step away.

Or step inside. Iris moved aside to let her in, and she crossed the threshold and set her bag just inside the door. The room she entered would have been appealing even if she wasn't comparing it to her accommodations from the night before. She had been expecting soft florals and pastels given the bungalow's woodsy, rural setting, but the living room was decorated in neutral shades of taupe, black, and silver. The clean lines and modern style of the furniture was saved from harshness by the bold splashes of jewel-toned throw pillows and abstract artwork. A fringed burgundy blanket was draped over the back of the couch, and an inviting stack of firewood sat next to the black-painted brick fireplace.

"I put a couple of meals in the freezer," Iris said as she led the way to the adjoining kitchen. She tapped on a piece of paper lying on the dark quartz countertop. "Just put them in the oven to reheat them, according to these cooking times. There's rice in the cupboard."

"Rice?" Casey asked. She looked at the few lines of directions Iris had written on the paper. That part looked easy enough.

She looked up again and saw Iris watching her with one of those unreadable expressions, as if she was carrying on an internal dialogue. This one must be funny, because she looked like she wanted to laugh.

"Yes, rice. Boil water and pour it in." Iris paused. "To boil water, you put water in a pan on the stove and turn on the burner. To turn on the burner—"

Casey laughed and waved her hand to make Iris stop. "I know that much at least," she said. "I've made tea before."

"Well, good," Iris said with a smile. "I was a little worried because you looked confused when I mentioned rice."

"I might not cook much, but it doesn't mean I can't cook. I certainly can make rice."

Iris looked as skeptical as Casey felt, but thankfully she didn't push the matter further. "The bedrooms are through here," she said, gesturing down the hall. "I put the gate there for the cat, and you and your dog can sleep in this room."

"Cat?" Casey asked, once again echoing the key word she picked out of Iris's sentences like she was a human highlighter.

"Yes, cat." Iris shook her head as she repeated her earlier phrasing as well. "The one I had with me on the ferry. She's been sleeping in the second bedroom's closet, so she should be fine having you here, as long as she gets her own space. She'll be having kittens soon, but not for—"

"*Kittens?*" Casey's voice sounded shrill to her own ears, and she cleared her throat. She could handle making rice and living with a cat, but she wasn't prepared to be a midwife during the delivery. "What am I supposed to do when she has them? Did you put that on your instruction sheet, too?"

"Of course," Iris said with a soothing tone. "Just boil some water. Put a pan on the stove, and fill it with water. Turn on the burner…"

Iris looked serious, and Casey wasn't sure if she was joking or not. What was she supposed to do with boiling water and a cat in labor?

Iris laughed and gave her shoulder a playful shove. "Don't worry. The vet will be here in the morning to check on her, and one of us is always here. If you notice her acting strangely, just come get me or Agatha or Leo. You said you wouldn't be here long, so most likely you'll be gone before the kittens come."

Iris's laughter faded, and Casey's concern about the cat shifted to the back of her mind. Yes, she'd be leaving soon. She needed to remember that. "You've given me incentive to work even faster than normal," she said, trying to make her voice sound light and teasing. "My boss will be grateful."

"I'd keep her in my house, but I already have three cats in there. Leo or I will feed her, and you probably won't even know she's here."

Casey sighed. Iris already had gotten a bad impression of her as an unfeeling seismologist, come to mock the island's inhabitants. Now she had probably crossed animal person off Casey's list of potentially positive traits.

"I don't mind sharing a house with a cat. I just don't have any experience with animals, and I don't want something to go wrong and have it be my fault."

Iris nodded as if accepting the explanation, but Casey wanted to offer more. She wasn't sure why Iris's opinion mattered, and she wasn't exactly happy about delving into her past, but she couldn't seem to help herself.

"My parents were divorced right after I was born, and my mother died when I was young. I went to live with my dad and grandparents, and when I asked them for a dog, they said no." Casey frowned as she tried to remember those first months after she had gone to live with them. The habit of avoidance was powerful, though. Even when she tried to access the memories on purpose, they grew hazy and her mind distracted her with thoughts of work and of the sadness in Iris's eyes while she listened. "They said pets were messy and too much responsibility. I eventually stopped asking, and I've never really been around animals since."

"I'm right up the path," Iris said, putting her hand on Casey's upper arm and giving her a squeeze. "Come get me if you're worried about anything."

The touch both soothed Casey and made her want to cry. She felt vulnerable here, around Iris and all her animals, and she wasn't sure why. She hated the feeling. Her childhood had made her strong. Educated and capable, independent and self-sufficient. So why did she feel weak? She needed to get off this island that was both too small and too expansive for comfort.

Iris let go of her and stepped back, as if sensing Casey's renewed resolve to leave.

"I've got to get back to work while there's still daylight," Casey said. She and the dog had hiked along one segment of the fault this morning, and she wanted to examine another chunk of it before dark. She couldn't forget why she was here.

Iris nodded, her expression a little distant again at the mention of Casey's job. Casey wasn't sure if it was because Iris still thought she was uncaring or if her work reminded Iris of the frightening earthquake she had experienced.

"Let me know if you need anything. If you want to take your dog with you, I'm sure Leo has finished with his bath by now."

Casey nodded her thanks and left Iris standing in the bungalow. She considered getting in her truck and leaving, but the dog had been useful this morning. The presence of another living being had given her an excuse to describe her observations out loud, and she had made several connections she might not have made if she had been alone and silent. In the interest of scientific breakthroughs, she had better keep him with her.

For science. Not for companionship.

She went back to the kennels and searched for Leo and her dog. She walked with purpose for a few steps before giving in to the wagging tails and eager noses pressed against the chain-link fences. She crouched by one of the runs and let a little black dog sniff her hand through the wire. It wiggled happily when she scratched its chin, and she felt an answering smile creep across her face. She went from kennel to kennel, stopping for a quick visit with each of the dogs and assessing any damage she could see.

Research. For when she helped repair the kennels.

She saw several areas where Iris and her helpers must have done quick patch jobs, and her mind automatically started to rearrange panels to reduce the number they'd have to replace. By the time she reached the end of the aisle, she had a blueprint in her mind. They might lose a few inches of space in most of the runs, but the difference wouldn't be noticeable.

Casey reached through the chain link to pet a small dog with frizzy tan hair. She didn't know one dog breed from another, but this little creature looked like she was a mix of several different types. None of her parts—from her tall ears to her long body to her short legs—seemed to match. When Casey straightened up and moved away from the kennel, the ragamuffin dog stood on her hind legs and whined.

Casey shook her head and walked away. She felt as if she could stay here for hours, talking to each animal and planning how to fix the kennels, but she had her own work to do. Iris needed her to help clear away branches and to do some minor repairs. A few hours a day, once it was too dark outside to do her regular job, were all she had to contribute in exchange for a temporary place to stay. Casey felt herself getting too involved. With Iris, with the dog Casey herself had rescued, and with these other animals. She couldn't get distracted from her study of the earthquake by the people and animals affected by it. She had tried to explain that to Iris on the ferry, and now she needed to convince herself again, as well.

Casey peered through a glass square on one of the doors leading off the aisle, and she saw Leo grooming her dog. He was standing on a low table, and Casey saw a large stainless-steel tub in the corner of the room. She went inside and was hit by the menthol smell of eucalyptus. She blinked a couple of times at the eye-watering aroma. She now had a clean dog and clear sinuses.

Leo looked up when she entered and smiled at her. "He's ready to go. He seems to be someone's dog, and he was very well-behaved during his bath."

"He looks great, Leo. Thank you." Casey set her sweatshirt and backpack on the floor and went over to stroke the dog's clean fur. He smiled at her with his tongue hanging out to one side. She wanted him to find his home again and she couldn't keep him with her, but she secretly hoped the owners wouldn't come looking for him until she was ready to leave the island. She scratched behind his ears in a way she had discovered that he loved. Maybe they could come for him after she had left, so she wouldn't really have to say good-bye.

"Have you named him?" Leo asked.

"No. Should I?"

"We always give our new residents names, but not the earthquake dogs." Leo put the shampoo and comb on a low shelf near the tub. "Iris is a bit superstitious about them because she wants to believe they're only here for a short time until their owners come. We've been identifying them based on where they were found, so we can remember easily if anyone phones about a missing pet. But you can name him if you want."

Casey had found the dog near Lime Kiln State Park, but she couldn't imagine calling him Lime Kiln every time she needed his attention. She pictured San Juan Island, with the late Jurassic, early Cretaceous Constitution Formation covering most of the land mass. "I found him where the Orcas Chert is exposed near the coastline, if that helps." She blinked away the map in her head and saw Leo watching her with his eyebrows pulled together, as if he was trying to figure her out. "The chert layer is older, and it's exposed in a few places on the island. It's a sedimentary rock, made of the silica-based skeletons of microscopic plankton called radiolarians, which dates it to the Triassic to early Jurassic eras."

Casey stopped herself from launching into a more detailed description of the island. Leo was studying her as she talked, as if he was seeing something beyond her words. Most people got a glazed look in their eyes when she started rambling about geology, but this was different, and Casey felt as exposed as the formation she was talking about. When she had chatted to Iris on the ferry, the talk of rocks and faults had been like flint—another type of chert—igniting a fire in Iris.

Why did people on this island seem to read more into her words than she meant to say?

"So you want to call him Chert?" Leo asked after the silence between them had stretched for too many seconds.

Casey shrugged. "Sure. Or Rover. Fido?"

Leo laughed loudly and patted her on the shoulder. "Chert it is. Are you taking this fellow rock hunting with you?"

"We're going on a hike," Casey said vaguely. She wasn't sure how Iris would react to the geology-related name, or to him being part of Casey's study of the island after the earthquake. "We have a few hours before it gets dark, and I'll be back to help around here as soon as the sun sets."

She lifted the dog off the table just as two small creatures careened into the room and ran into her legs. Both Casey and the dog jumped backward.

"What are...oh, they're baby goats." Casey watched the two brown-and-white spotted goats scamper around the wash-room. Leo rescued her backpack from one of them when it started chewing on a strap.

"Iris's Twins," Leo said. "They can't resist an open door, so be sure to close up tight when you leave the bungalow."

Casey picked up her sweatshirt and shook a bunch of little brown pellets off it. "How cute," she said, but she didn't sound convincing even to herself. She remembered quiet goats from her petting zoo memory, but they were nothing like these exuberant kids. Chert watched them with his tail held low, obviously as uncertain about them as Casey was. One of the little goats jumped up on its hind legs and planted its front hooves on Casey's thigh. It didn't weigh much, but when the full force of its body was concentrated in such a small surface area, Casey nearly fell over. She was going to have two perfectly shaped hoofprints on her thigh tomorrow.

She tried to match Leo's indulgent smile as the goats flung themselves out of the room again like they were in a pinball machine. She was feeling overwhelmed by the day, from waking up in the truck to finding the dog to coming to this place that was overrun with animals. Most of all, to being around Iris who was at once arousing and unlike anyone Casey had ever known. She needed to get out in the field and find some peace and quiet in order to process the day's events—and those were two things Casey rarely sought on purpose.

"We'll see you later, Leo," she said. She led Chert out the door, and once outside he pulled her toward her truck and jumped in as soon as she opened the door, as if he owned her and the vehicle. She got the LIDAR map of the island out of her glove compartment and compared it to a regular road map to find an access point to the fault she wanted to study.

"Ready to go?" she asked her passenger, and he wagged his tail in response.

❖

By the time Casey was finished with her two jobs, she was exhausted. She had worried about being able to sleep without the distractions of the city, but as she sat on the couch and watched the fire in the fireplace burn itself out, she felt her body relaxing and her mind drifting out of focus.

She'd had a productive day along the fault line, snapping photographs and taking notes as she examined the slight shifts that supported the estimated location of the fault. She had come back to the shelter and labored side by side with Agatha and Leo by the artificial light of the kennels as they shifted panels and repaired damaged wire. She had worked up a sweat trying to keep up with Agatha's pace and to keep her mind off Iris, who always managed to be fixing a kennel far from Casey's. She had spent a disconcerting amount of time looking for her, though, and admiring the mouthwatering way she fit in her jeans, the gentle way she interacted with the animals, and the precise way she stitched broken fences back together.

Casey even liked the way Iris laughed at the antics of the goats as they bounded like deer from person to person, chewing on tools and pooping on anything Casey set on the ground.

Casey still wasn't sure about those goats.

She yawned and stretched, pulling the burgundy throw around her shoulders and leaning against Chert's sleeping form. The house still smelled good from dinner, and Casey inhaled the lingering scents of lime and cilantro. The chicken had been delicious, and the tastes made her imagine Iris cooking the meal and moving around her kitchen with a confidence Casey didn't feel. Her rice had been unpleasantly crunchy in the center, but she had eaten every bite of it and the flavorful chicken.

She looked behind her and saw the gray cat peering at her through the slats of the baby gate. Chert had put his nose against the gate when he first got in the bungalow, and the cat had observed him from her bedroom doorway for a few minutes before retreating under the bed again. Chert had lost interest and had returned to Casey's side.

She sighed and tossed the throw over the back of the couch, heading toward the bedroom with the dog right behind her. She collapsed on the soft bed and pulled the covers over her as Chert settled himself against her legs. She would make it through her time on the islands without any problem as long as she kept herself too busy to think of anything except work and as long as the cat didn't go into labor.

And as long as she could keep herself from crossing the tiny yard separating her from Iris's house, her bedroom, and her too-enticing body.

Chapter Eight

Iris was in the kennels before dawn the next morning, having barely slept the night before. She yawned as she scooped a hefty dose of ground coffee into a paper filter and switched on the machine. She hadn't had a good night's sleep since the quake, and Casey's closeness wasn't helping. She had tossed and turned, finally giving up and coming to the kennels. There was always work to do here, and she might as well be useful if she wasn't going to be asleep.

She brought her coffee into the infirmary and set it on the metal table as she gathered bandages and ointment from the cupboards. She let herself into Jack's run and sat next to his bed, where he lay wagging his tail with a thumping noise against the cushion. She gently took one of his paws and cut the bandage away, inspecting the small cuts before she applied a thick layer of ointment and rebandaged the wounds.

Luckily, he was patient about the procedure since she had to clean and check his paws every day. She was on the third one when she looked up and saw Casey in the doorway, watching her silently.

"You're up early," Iris said.

"I couldn't sleep." Casey came into the room with Chert close behind. She sat down next to the run and Chert dropped at her side like a shadow. "What happened to these dogs?"

"The earthquake. This one got out of his run and walked over broken glass from the office window." Iris tilted her head in Gus's direction. "And he cut himself on a piece of wire that snapped when a branch hit it."

Iris caught herself before she added an uncalled-for comment about Casey studying their wounds as part of her earthquake research. She was tired and cranky, but she didn't need to be rude. She saw the sympathy in Casey's expression and in the careful way she reached through the fence and scratched Gus's chin.

Iris finished wrapping Jack's paw and carried her bundle of bandages out of his run, balancing them in one arm as she unlatched Gus's gate.

Casey stepped over and opened the door for Iris. "Do you need help with him?"

Iris heard the hesitation in Casey's voice, but Gus's wounds were difficult to dress with only one person doing the work. "Actually, yes. It's usually a two-person job, but I was here early and thought I'd get it done before Agatha and Leo get here. I'd appreciate the help, if you really don't mind."

Casey followed her into the run and shut the door behind her, keeping Chert from squeezing into the narrow kennel with them. She knelt next to Gus and stroked his head.

"What do I do?"

"Just hold him still. Like this"—Iris gathered Gus close to her, with his head resting in the crook of her elbow—"keeping his head turned. He won't try to bite me, but he tries to grab the bandages."

She released him and watched Casey try to mimic her hold. Iris was tempted to physically move Casey's hands and arms into the right position, but she kept her hands busy rerolling a length of gauze instead. The bandage had a nubbly texture, but the imagined touch of her fingers on Casey's smooth skin over-rode reality, and Iris swore she could feel Casey instead of the rough cotton.

As soon as Casey seemed to have a somewhat comfort-able grip on Gus, Iris removed the old bandage and checked the wound. She worked quickly because she wasn't sure what Casey would do if the dog started to struggle. As it was, she seemed determined not to look anywhere even close to the wound.

"He looks good," Iris said, hoping to reassure Casey with her words. "The area around the stitches doesn't show any sign of infection. Pretty soon we'll be able to take the bandages off and let the wound heal in the open."

Iris taped the edges of the new bandage and wrapped it se-curely. "He'll be wearing one of those humiliating cones before the end of the week. You can let him go now."

Casey released her hold on Gus and smiled at Iris. "I sup-pose all the other dogs will laugh at him."

"Of course. And they'll post embarrassing pictures on his Facebook page. Thank you for holding him. You did a good job."

Casey gave a derisive snort as she came out of the run. "Hardly. You're the one who did the work. I'm not used to all of this. Taking care of animals, I mean. Or people either, I guess."

Iris put her supplies away and washed her hands. "You're doing great. You seem to be a natural at it."

"I wouldn't go that far, but I am having more fun than I expected. I even enjoy doing the manual labor of fixing the kennels."

"You can have that part of it," Iris said with a distracted smile. She was still thinking about Casey's admission that she didn't have much experience taking care of anyone but herself. Her type of existence was far removed from Iris's, whose entire life seemed to be spent caring for other creatures and people. She couldn't imagine what it would be like not to be accountable to anyone or anything. There would be more freedom, and Iris purposefully kept her thoughts away from all the trips and hobbies she'd be able to pursue if she were as unencumbered as Casey. Not worth the trade. That life would be too sterile for her.

Casey was in the middle of explaining something to her when Iris finally brought her attention back to the present.

"Wait…what?"

"I said I have an idea about the kennels," Casey said. "I think we can rearrange them so you won't have to replace as many panels. The runs will be a little smaller—"

"No," Iris said with a snap in her voice. "The dogs need as much room as we can give them."

"The runs will be a little smaller," Casey repeated herself, "but only a few inches at most. I know they need space, but you could save hundreds of dollars if you can still use most of the panels."

They glared at each other in silence for a few seconds. Iris had been feeling more generous toward Casey after watching her with the dogs and seeing how much she was helping out, but her attempts to take over and change the shelter were out of line. Casey was right. She wasn't used to taking care of animals, and she had no idea what it would mean for Iris to rearrange her entire kennel. Especially now, after the earthquake.

"You don't understand how difficult it is to shift the dogs around. They need consistency, and anything we do to disrupt their routine causes stress. We're better off repairing everything we can and replacing what's necessary."

"Do they really need a routine, or do you?" Casey asked.

Iris raised her eyebrows. Casey might not realize how much her words were a trigger for Iris, but Iris heard an implied insult in her question. "I can adapt if I need to," she said. She gave Jack a pat as she walked by his run. Chert and Casey got to their feet at the same time.

"Let's start over," Casey said with a sigh that sounded as resigned to their constant bickering as Iris felt. "If you have a piece of paper, I can show you what I was thinking."

Iris silently got a notepad and pencil out of a drawer, and then watched as Casey sketched out a plan for the kennels. Even while Iris was thinking about how much work it would be to disrupt dogs and reorganize her carefully orchestrated setup, she couldn't keep from imagining where each dog would be most comfortable in the new arrangement. *If* she agreed to it, that is.

She leaned her elbow on the table and pointed at one of the clusters of kennels Casey had drawn. "We have a few dogs that seem to feel more secure if they have several dogs close to them. We can't really give them a sense of being in a pack when the runs are side by side, but we could with them arranged in these clusters, if we move these runs over here…"

Casey erased part of her sketch and redrew the runs using Iris's suggestion. "Like that?" she asked.

Iris picked up the drawing and studied it carefully, picturing it in three-dimensional space. It could work.

"I'm sorry I'm so quick to get angry," she said, putting the paper on the table again and forcing herself to meet Casey's calm gray gaze.

"You're under a lot of stress," Casey said. She touched Iris briefly on the shoulder. "We both are, and it makes tempers short. I'm sorry, too. You know more about dogs and running a kennel than I do—"

"But you came up with a solution that might work." Iris tapped the drawing with one finger as she stepped away in what she hoped was a casual manner. She couldn't deny that Casey had a powerful effect on her. Right now, it was being expressed as irritation, but she was certain she could find other outlets for the buildup of energy she felt when she was near Casey. Still, rearranging the kennels was one thing, but changing the pattern of her life was something else entirely. She'd start small. "We can try this with the runs along the back wall since a couple of them are empty."

"Great," Casey said. "I'll get the tools we need, if you move the dogs."

Iris nodded and left the infirmary, dropping off her mug of now-cooled coffee in the office and grabbing some leashes. She quickly transferred the two dogs to the empty runs next to Jack and Gus, leaving the four dogs happily chewing on rawhide bones as she went to help Casey.

They started to dismantle the runs in silence, and Casey was the first to break it.

"You're lucky to live in such a beautiful place," she said. "It seems like I find another gorgeous view around every corner."

Iris was holding a panel steady while Casey stood on a ladder and unscrewed it from the metal post. She cleared her throat before she could speak. She wasn't about to admit that the view she had just been admiring was Casey herself.

"Yes, the islands are lovely. I try not to take this place for granted, but I can't always find time to get out and explore." She shifted so she wasn't staring directly at Casey's backside. If she was going to be expected to string words together into sentences, she couldn't have such an enticing distraction right in front of her. "You're the lucky one, because your job lets you travel a lot."

Casey glanced down at her and shrugged. "I don't really do much fieldwork anymore, so this is a treat." She shook her head with a frown. "I don't mean the earthquake was a treat, I meant—"

Iris patted her on the calf, ignoring the urge to rest her hand against the strong muscles she felt there. "I know. I'm sorry I make you watch every word you say."

Casey nodded and turned her attention back to the panel while she talked. "When I got my first job after grad school, I ended up in a position that does more data interpretation than fieldwork, but I miss seeing things before they get reduced to black-and-white data. I enjoy what I do, and I believe it's important work, but I was glad when my new boss asked me to come out here and observe firsthand."

Casey tugged the panel free and came down the ladder to move it to the next side of the run. She grinned at Iris before she climbed again. "I took a year off between college and graduate school to hike the Pacific Crest Trail. My dad and grandparents weren't happy that I wasn't hurrying through my degree, but I convinced them I was doing field research for a scholarly article."

"Did you get published?" Iris asked.

"Nah. I have tons of notes, but they're mostly numbers. Types of rocks I found, how many miles I walked, that sort of thing. Lots of lists."

"You did the whole trail at once? How long did it take?" Iris wouldn't have been able to desert her parents for an extended length of time, and once she was in school and then at the shelter, she'd had too many responsibilities to leave. The sort of freedom Casey had was alien to her. Something to be desired, but not something she would sacrifice her present life to have.

"It took me a little over four months," Casey said. She leaned her elbows on the ladder and looked lost in memories for a moment. "I kind of hurried through it, to be honest. It's the kind of trip that invites introspection, and I don't think I'm very good at that. I pushed myself pretty hard, but it was worth doing."

"I've always wanted to walk the trail. What an amazing accomplishment." Iris could imagine Casey striding over mountains like they were nothing more than bumps in the road. She couldn't picture herself anywhere along the trail no matter how hard she tried. Maybe it would be a place with too much room for thought, where she would be too inclined to be reflective. Casey wanted to avoid it, and Iris might get lost in it.

Casey hopped off the ladder and laid her fingers on Iris's cheek, turning her face so Iris had to look at her. "Lots of people hike it in sections. Not everyone can take four or five months away from home, but most can manage a couple weeks at a time. It's worth seeing."

Somehow, when Casey touched her, a mental image of herself standing on a ridge and looking over a pine-filled valley flashed through Iris's mind. Casey made the idea of walking the trail in segments sound possible, while Iris seemed conditioned to think everything was impossible. She rested her hand over Casey's for a moment, and then they both dropped the contact as if on cue.

Casey turned away and propped the panel against the wall, and Iris had a few seconds to compose herself. She had felt the expected electricity in Casey's touch, but she hadn't tried to fight it this time. She was accustomed to not having dreams, but Casey didn't seem to think any were out of reach.

Was Casey good for her, or was Iris setting herself up for disappointment if the hopes stirring inside her didn't come true?

"You'll have to give me some of your lists if I go," Iris said, keeping the mood lighthearted. "So I'll know where to go and what to pack."

Casey laughed. "Whatever you do, don't take a geologist's advice on what to bring. Most hikers start out on the trail with too much stuff, and gradually get rid of the excess. I started out light, and collected rocks along the way. By the time I reached the Canadian border, my pack weighed a ton and my pockets were full."

"I don't think rock collecting will be a problem for me," Iris said with a grin. "I'll just keep a few with me, in case I need to scare off a rattlesnake."

"Good idea," Casey said. "Although, I have a feeling you'd collect wild animals like I collected rocks."

"You're probably right," Iris said, pulling one of the loose panels into its new position. "Then I'll need to have you come back to the islands and build me more kennels."

"You've got a deal," Casey said with a wink.

Iris smiled, accepting her words in the teasing way they were meant, even though her heart beat a little faster at the thought.

CHAPTER NINE

We could move Trixie over here. She'll have more privacy in the corner. Or maybe she'd be okay with Duncan next to her. I think they got along fine when they first came here..."

Casey had her palms on the desk, near Iris's forearm, and she leaned over to watch Iris pencil in names and then erase them again as she completed the new kennel schematic. They had finished two of the new kennel configurations, and Casey was happy to see that she had been correct about how much money and repair time the new clusters would save.

She had come to realize that Iris had been right, too. Casey had expected the process to be a simple one—switch the panels, pop some dogs in, and voila. Done. But some dogs had spent the morning barking, some pacing, and others hiding in their shelters and refusing to come out.

Casey glanced toward the run nearest to the office, where a svelte hound was baying loudly. "Will the dogs be all right? I shouldn't have tried to mess with your system."

"They'll settle quickly, once we have them in their new places and give them some food," Iris said, her voice slightly raised to be heard over the hound's woeful song. She patted Casey's hand where it rested on the table. "Your plan works, and I think it will make feeding time go more smoothly as well. The process of change is difficult, but it will be worth it once we're done."

Casey wrenched her attention away from the feel of Iris's hand on hers long enough to see the surprised expression on Iris's face as she made her last statement. "I thought you were just being stubborn this morning, when I brought up my idea," Casey said. "But now I completely understand why you didn't want to upset the status quo."

Iris stopped writing. "That was part of it. I guess I'm not used to someone telling me what to do." She held up her hand to stop Casey's protests before she could interrupt. "I know you didn't mean it that way. It was just a trigger for me."

She looked like she was struggling to find the right words to say, so Casey kept silent and waited for Iris to speak again.

"I had parents who were overprotective and tried to control everything I did—mostly to keep me safe and close to them, but still…And then girlfriends who never seemed to approve of the way I lived my life." Iris paused and stared out the window toward the path leading to her house. "I've sort of isolated myself here. I'm not alone, but Agatha and Leo are happy to keep everything the same. Or to make changes, if I suggest them. I don't have anyone here who tries to tell me what to do."

"And when I made it sound as if you had the kennels set up the wrong way, you went into self-defense mode." Casey nodded. "I get it. I'd have reacted the same way if you had told me a different way to deploy my seismometers."

Iris laughed. "Well, I've been meaning to bring it up…"

"I figured you were going to work on a schematic for them as soon as you finished this one for the kennels." Casey's grin faded. "I understand what you mean about isolating yourself from any chance of being told how to run your life. My dad and grandparents had definite ideas about what I needed to study, where I should go to college, and everything else. I've spent my life either trying to please them or trying to get away and make my own decisions. It's exhausting to be on that particular seesaw."

"It is," Iris said with a nod. "I don't want my past to keep me from recognizing good suggestions when I hear them, though, so thank you for bringing this up."

Casey reached over and smoothed back a loose strand of Iris's hair, pulling away before she let her index finger follow the gentle curve of Iris's ear. "I'll be more sensitive about this trigger when I make suggestions in the future."

Iris turned to face her, shifting out of reach as she did so. "Don't tell me you have *more* suggestions," she said with a look of exaggerated horror.

"Tons of them. But let's get this project finished first. I know it's a lot to take on, especially when you have so much other work to do."

And when Casey had work of her own. She had helped set this course in motion, and she would have to leave Iris in the middle of it. She'd have Agatha and Leo to help, of course, and they were already working on the third set of kennels, but Casey decided she'd stay at the shelter longer than she'd planned and help them finish.

"You need to go," Iris said in a distracted sounding voice. She looked back at her paper and made a shooing motion, as if she had heard Casey's thoughts. "I'll be able to think this through better if you aren't so close…"

Iris paused, but still avoided eye contact. "I mean, Agatha and I are accustomed to shifting the dogs around whenever we get a new one. We'll be able to figure this out pretty quickly, and by the time you get back tonight, the place should be back to normal and quiet. Relatively quiet."

Casey backed up a step, not bothering to hide the smile she felt tugging against her mouth since Iris was staring at her paper. Casey saw a hint of a blush on the back of Iris's neck and she had an overwhelming urge to kiss her and feel the heat of it burn against her lips. She had been mesmerized by the feel of Iris's skin this morning, and had sought any excuse to touch her and see if the connection she felt dissipated or got stronger. Scientific inquiry, and nothing more. Although caressing Iris's cheek hadn't exactly been a scientific move.

She had been concerned only with her response to Iris, wondering how it could keep increasing with each featherlight touch, and she hadn't stopped to consider that *she* might be affecting Iris, too. Although she wanted to stay and explore this new theory, she knew Iris was about to have a chaotic and loud morning as she got her dogs settled. Casey would probably be more help if she left her in peace than if she remained and couldn't control her wandering hands.

"We'll go, then," Casey said, laying her hand on Chert's head. "But I'll check in later. If you need me to help, I'll come back."

Iris looked at her then. "All right. Be safe out there, you two."

Casey nodded and left before her scientific experiment extended to include kissing. Her mind was still on the morning's conversation with Iris as she got in her truck, and she changed her itinerary at the last minute and drove to the ferry dock instead of into the interior of San Juan.

She and Chert waited in the cab since the ride to Lopez Island took less than an hour, and she took the opportunity to review the notes she had made so far. She had collected pages of information for her report to the lab, but she also had two spiral notebooks filled with less professional scribblings about the geology of the islands and her appreciation of them. These ramblings weren't useful for her job, but she had felt compelled to write down some of the conversations she had with Chert while in the field, as well as the silent ones she had when she imagined playing tour guide for Iris and showing her the fascinating layers beneath her home.

Casey tossed those notes into the glove compartment before she drove off the ferry and onto the island where she had first gotten a glimpse of Iris and her string of animals. If she had known then that she would be staying at Iris's place while she was on San Juan, she might not have been too surprised—until she found out that she wasn't going to be staying in Iris's bed, but in the cottage next door, with animals and a part-time job as kennel volunteer. That part would have made her past self laugh in disbelief.

Casey patted Chert. Here she was, no matter how unexpectedly. She drove along the small, paved road that was heavily encroached by fir trees and ferns until she saw a decrepit sign pointing toward a pothole-filled gravel road. She bumped along in her poor truck, and Chert hopped onto the passenger-side floor in protest against the rough ride. Fifteen minutes of slow going got her to the UW satellite station.

She sat in her truck for a moment, marveling at the difference between this substation and the university's huge cement and steel lab that covered an entire city block. Iris's kennel looked more state-of-the-art than this place. In fact, Casey was surprised it hadn't been one of the first buildings to fall during the earthquake.

She got out of the truck with Chert and walked to the small tan metal building. The front door was propped open with a wedge-shaped piece of plastic, but she stood on the porch and knocked. The structure looked like nothing more important than a garden shed from the outside, but inside it was full of clutter, chattering data-collection machines, and haphazardly strewn instruments. Muddy boots were lined up near the door, and the three desks that were in use were covered with as many personal items as work-related ones—photos, piles of nondescript-looking rocks, and action figures from comics and science fiction series.

A young man came out of one of the back rooms—presumably a kitchen or break room since he was carrying a cup of coffee and a doughnut. He put them down on a desk and walked over to her. Casey smiled and shook his hand, wondering if he was one of the people she had emailed in the past. She and her teammates would occasionally send instructions to the satellites, asking them to move instruments or double-check suspicious readings.

Sort of the same thing she had done with Iris this morning—hand her a schematic, and then leave her to do the actual work. Iris was hands-on with everything in her shelter, just like this man was on the island. He was dressed for working outdoors, in a red plaid flannel shirt, tan waterproof jacket, and brown duck boots. He bent down to pet Chert, not seeming surprised that she had brought a dog to the station.

"I'm Casey Radnor," she said, "and this is Chert."

"Great name for a dog! I'm Ian. You're the fieldworker from the big lab, aren't you? C'mon back. Do you want some coffee? A doughnut?"

"Yes, and yes, please. I can get them if you point the way."

"Right back here."

She followed him to a surprisingly tidy kitchen where she poured cream and sugar in a cup of coffee and chose a maple bar out of a bakery box while Ian gave Chert a piece of glazed doughnut. Then they went back to his desk in the far corner of the main room. He took a stack of books off a chair and indicated for her to sit.

She gestured at the several empty desks. "I thought there would be more of you working here. We must keep you busy with all the requests for readings and field notes we send."

Ian shrugged. "We're short staffed, as always. We're part-time most of the year, and overtime after a big event like this one. I'd ask in a hopeful voice if you were here to fill in, but I know you're on assignment. We're under orders to help you, but not to put you to work for us."

Casey laughed and leaned back in her chair, letting the relaxed vibe of the station seep inside her. She hadn't realized how little fieldwork she really did now, until she had talked to Iris about it this morning. She had intentionally chosen jobs that took her deep into stainless-steel labs instead of deep into the forest.

She shook her head to get her father's voice out of it. He had been derisive when she told him she was planning to study geology. Her frequent appearance in respected journals and her jobs in high-tech, high-profile labs had mollified him a little. But he wasn't here now. And even if he were here, she'd have the same thing to say to Ian.

"I'd like to see more of this island, so if you don't mind, maybe I can tag along with someone today. And if that person happens to need an extra pair of hands to work…well, I won't tell the big lab if you won't."

Ian joined in Casey's laughter. "I'm not going to refuse an offer like that. I wanted to walk a fault line at Aleck Bay, and if we hurry, we'll be there for low tide. Do the two of you mind getting a little muddy?"

Casey translated his fieldwork-speak to mean that by the end of the day, she and Chert would probably be covered in mud and slime from head to toe. Or paw. She grinned. "We don't mind at all."

Chapter Ten

Iris wrapped her scarf more snugly around her neck and turned to a fresh page in her notebook. She had a tidy and well-appointed office in her house, complete with a spacious desk, handy reference books, and an ergonomically designed and very cushy chair, but she did most of her work out here, on the small patch of lawn behind the shelter's office. Her office was where she went when she needed to organize things, whether it was her color-coded files or the huge calendar tacked to the wall. When she needed inspiration for her work, she came outside.

She pulled her bright yellow knit cap lower over her ears and wondered if Casey was keeping warm wherever she was. She didn't seem to have a lot of cold-weather clothes with her and she had left this morning wearing only jeans and a sweatshirt, but she seemed unfazed by the elements. She seemed at home out in the world, comfortable with whatever Mother Nature presented to her.

Iris blew on her fingers to warm them and tried to turn her thoughts inward, off Casey and onto an imagined spring morning. She sketched an Easter basket overflowing with candy and plastic grass—picturing the bright, clear colors she would use in the final drawing—and started to list words alongside it.

Eventually, the words tangled with each other and traded places until they became a poem. She wrote it down quickly, before it vanished from her mind, and then she turned to a new page. On this one, she drew a cartoon rabbit searching under furniture and in clothes drawers for Easter eggs. A humorous verse about not forgetting where one had hidden the eggs was quickly formed and captured on paper.

She felt a tug on the end of her scarf and she absently reached down to pet one of the Twins and pull the fringe out of its mouth while she moved to the next blank page. She had the outline of a couple walking hand in hand along a rocky shoreline and a romantic poem splashed across the paper before she realized what she was doing. Easter. The elaborate chart hanging in her office said this month was the time to create greeting cards for Easter.

The romantic card was a good one, even though it wasn't on today's agenda. She tried to refocus on spring, but another image came to her and she drew it quickly. Another couple—too far away to identify—stood close together on a ferry, with a backdrop of wheeling gulls and fir-covered islands. A free verse poem about traveling together through life flowed from her pencil as if the lead had turned to running water. A third card idea came just as easily. Why not? She usually sent her cards in batches, anyway.

Three was enough of a diversion. She wished the inspiration had struck two months ago, when she had struggled to write cards for Valentine's Day. She usually loved the regularity of her work, with seasons and holidays mapped out and marching in regimented order through her days. She rarely was tempted to stray from her schedule, but she couldn't stop the ideas from popping into her thoughts.

She paused with a soothingly empty page in front of her and watched the two goats jumping on a series of stumps and planks that she and Leo had set out for them. She loved the little creatures because they were able to force smiles and laughter from her, even when she didn't think she had them in her. Casey had done the same thing, bringing a sense of playfulness into Iris's life, but she wasn't sure how welcome Casey's influence was. Nice while it lasted, but not something to rely on.

Iris let her thoughts settle on Casey for a brief time because she was tired of fighting them. Casey had only been here for a few days, and Iris had no idea what she did or where she went during the daylight hours, but she had somehow become part of the shelter. With her help, the property was nearly back to its pre-earthquake state. She had somehow managed to minimize the number of destroyed panels they needed to replace because of her inspired rearrangement of the kennels.

Iris had been hesitant to switch from her orderly and linear rows of dog runs to Casey's vision of clustered kennels, but the change had worked. The new layout would save them money and it even opened up more space for new animals. Leo couldn't stop talking about Casey's ingenuity, and even the normally recalcitrant Agatha seemed enamored of her. The dogs agreed, too, and they clamored for Casey's attention whenever she walked into the shelter.

Iris wasn't sure how she felt. Casey was distractingly attractive and undeniably helpful. She wasn't as coldly scientific and distant as Iris had originally thought, although she sometimes wished Casey was more disappointing as a human being. Then Iris would have been glad to see her go. Now she knew there would be a void when Casey left.

One of the Twins trotted over to her and butted her in the thigh before trying to grab her pencil. Iris laughed and held it out of reach until he gave up and ran back to his sister. Iris loved the peace of her shelter and the predictability of her work, but would it seem as adequate once Casey had left?

Casey was changing more than the kennels around here. She was interesting and energetic, daring and confident. Every quality Iris lacked. She had managed to keep from feeling that something was missing from her life—from *her*—and focus instead on her writing and caring for the animals, but Casey was so deeply and vibrantly everything that Iris wasn't that she couldn't ignore what she was missing anymore.

She started writing again, with no illustrations this time. She wanted to censor what was falling onto the page, to stop the movement of her pencil across the rough sketchpad, but she could no more have halted the earth's movement during the quake. She gave up and set the poem free. It wasn't suitable for her greeting cards, but maybe it would leave her alone if she put it down on paper.

When she finally stopped, she looked up and saw Casey watching her. "Hey," she said.

"Hey, back," Casey said with a smile. "I didn't mean to interrupt. You looked very intense."

"Work," Iris said, holding up her notepad. What she had just been writing had nothing to do with her job, but she didn't mention that. "I write greeting cards."

"Really?" Casey came over and crouched down beside Iris's folding chair. "I've never met a greeting card writer before. Do you like it?"

Iris paused. She liked the routine nature of the job and the easy way the poetry flowed when required to do so. The companies she worked with had very specific requirements, and it was easy for her to meet them. There were no surprises, no unexpected holidays or sudden changes in the expectations for a Christmas or birthday card. Would any of those aspects of her job sound appealing to Casey? Probably not.

"I enjoy being creative," she said slowly, trying to think about the cards she had written today and not the poem she'd just finished. "I can write something funny or something serious, depending on my mood. And they're so short I can fit them around my schedule here in the kennels, which is good because they pay for this place."

"Can I see one of them?" Casey asked, gesturing at the notepad.

Iris hesitated. She usually was happy to let others read her work, often asking Leo or Agatha to look through them before she sent her submissions, but the sketchpad felt tainted by the raw emotions from the longer poem. She had no good reason to hide Easter eggs from Casey, though, so she flipped to one of the earlier cards and handed her the pad. "I have to send them in months before the actual holidays, and I'm doing spring cards now."

Casey read the poem and smiled. "You draw really well," she said. "I've learned the basics of drawing for my job, but I don't have a natural talent for it like you do. Aw, cute bunny!"

Before Iris could stop her, Casey turned another page and got to the poem she'd just written. Casey's expression grew more serious and she sat on the ground. Iris could see her scan the words quickly, and then reread the poem more slowly. What should she say? That she was experimenting with a more serious line of cards? That the words of regret and inadequacy and loneliness were for a Halloween card because they were the scariest ones she could imagine?

She remained silent, hoping Casey would just read it and forget about it.

No such luck.

"Wow," Casey said. The simple word melted into an audible exhale. Iris was embarrassed because she felt exposed by the poem, but a small part of her was thrilled to have touched Casey.

"This is…wow. You're amazing, Iris. I mean, the cards are good, but this is special. Do you publish your poems, too?"

"Goodness, no," Iris said, although the statement was only true in the present, not the past. She had been required to publish two chapbooks during grad school at the Pacific Lutheran University, and she had won several contests only because her professors had entered her poems in them. "I specialized in poetry when I got my MFA from PLU in Tacoma, but I just write those occasionally for fun. I'm only interested in publishing my cards."

"Can't you do both?" Casey finally looked away from the poem and at her, and Iris took the opportunity to take her notepad back. She tried to make her movement casual, and not snatch the pad like she was grabbing her soul away from Casey.

"Why bother? Greeting cards sell better, and I earn a steady income. Serious poetry won't put dog food in the bowls."

Iris was trying to make a joke, but she felt a coil of tension in her shoulders. She stretched her neck unobtrusively, forcing her muscles to relax. She wasn't a stranger to the feeling that she was falling short somehow, in her life and career choices. In fact, the poem had been about that very issue. But she wasn't going to let Casey know how personal the poem actually was, and she sure as hell wasn't going to let Casey add her endorsement to the similar opinions expressed by Iris's former girlfriends. She hadn't changed who she was for them, and she wouldn't change for Casey. Of course, none of them had encouraged Iris to write more poetry, but still…

"Why can't you do both?" Casey repeated. "Keep doing the cards, because you're obviously good at writing them, but send some of these other poems to magazines or book publishers or wherever poets send their stuff."

"I'm happy with the way I'm living my life right now," Iris said, hearing her voice rise in volume even though she wasn't getting louder on purpose. She needed to convince someone— either Casey or herself, she didn't know which—that she was satisfied with the way things were. "I'm not the type who keeps wanting more. Those kinds of people either are disappointed when life doesn't go the way they expect it to, or they just keep wanting more and are never happy with what they have."

Casey watched her with a frown. "You missed the third option, Iris. Sometimes people who want more make their dreams come true."

Iris shook her head, not because she didn't believe what Casey was saying but because she wasn't convinced Casey believed it. She had only told Iris about a small part of her childhood, but she had been able to fill in some gaps. She imagined Casey felt lonely and sad as a child, after losing her mother when she was very young, and then going to live with a father and grandparents who sounded cold and uninviting. Even now, watching the way she was tentative around the animals even though they responded well to her, Iris had the feeling that Casey wasn't accustomed to expecting unconditional love. But she really didn't know Casey well at all. Maybe she had found some sort of fulfillment that Iris wasn't seeing.

"Have you made your dreams come true, Casey?"

Casey leaned away from Iris's chair and averted her eyes. She looked toward the office, at the goats, toward the sky that was obscured by a solid blanket of gray—avoiding Iris's gaze, but not focusing on anything in particular. "I have a great new job. I wouldn't have gotten it if I had been complacent and settled into my old one. The lab at UW is spectacular, and I'm making new friends in the city. So yes, I've reached some career and personal goals, and I'll keep striving toward new ones." She looked at Iris, and her eyes were the color of the clouds and just as unfathomable. "But I don't have your gift with words. Poems like this one should be shared, not hidden away in notepads."

"Maybe I write them for myself," Iris said. Casey's compliments should make her proud, not make her want to run away. "Maybe I don't want anyone else to read them."

Casey opened her mouth as if to say something, but she closed it again. After a few moments of silence, she spoke. "Do those goats have names? I've only heard them called the Twins."

Iris had been busily erecting emotional walls between herself and Casey, but the abrupt shift in topic made her smile. "Are you subtly changing the subject?"

"How you choose to either use or hide your talent is none of my business," Casey said. "I was making you uncomfortable and I'm sorry."

"Holmes and Watson," Iris said. "The goats. Because they examine everything they find lying around like they're searching for clues to solve an important case. They're very thorough."

"Yes, I've noticed," Casey said with a shake of her head. "Every job I do around here takes twice as long as it should because they keep grabbing tools and running off with them."

Iris laughed, surprised as always by Casey's ability to make her shift her emotions in a heartbeat. The move from upset to laughter was a welcome one. "Apology accepted, by the way. I guess my poetry is too personal to share and I'm protective of it."

Casey nodded as if satisfied with the explanation, but Iris wasn't. Why hadn't she tried to publish some of her poems after grad school? Her professors had been encouraging, and she had a thick folder of poetry she thought was pretty good hidden in the back of her file cabinet. She had faced rejection before, especially when she had first started writing greeting cards, and although she didn't like the feeling, it hadn't immobilized her. She hadn't been lying when she said she was happy with the way her life was going, for the most part.

Why start chasing dreams of tomorrows and losing all of her todays?

She was tempted to reopen the subject with Casey and maybe figure out what was holding her back, but Leo came through the office's back door.

"Iris, there are some people here who have lost a dog. A little girl and her parents. They're in the parking lot."

Iris jumped to her feet, always thrilled with the possibility of finding one of her animals a home. "Want to come?" she asked Casey. "You might get to witness a wonderful reunion."

Casey had gotten to her feet as well, but more slowly than Iris. Iris felt her enthusiasm fade a little and she felt Casey's sudden tension as acutely as she had felt her own earlier in their conversation. She put her hand on Casey's forearm and slid her palm down Casey's cotton sweatshirt until their fingers were entwined. The kennels, Leo, and her own struggles with her poetry disappeared, and all she felt was Casey's skin against her own. Her hand was warm and rough from drying autumn weather and her work on the dog run. Her fingers gripped Iris's tightly, and Iris felt Casey's need to be close, if only for this brief moment.

"I have a lot of dogs here, and there are even more at other shelters. The chance of it being Chert's owners...But if they are..."

Casey nodded with a jerky movement. "I know. I'm all right."

And in a flash, she was. Iris wasn't sure what went on in Casey's mind, but she went from panic to serene without any in-between. Casey gave Iris's hand a squeeze, as if Iris was the one who needed comforting.

"Let's go. I'm looking forward to seeing this side of your job."

Iris missed the physical contact with Casey as soon as their hands separated, but the sudden emotional distance was even more heartbreaking. She felt loneliness wash over her, and she wasn't sure if it was her own or Casey's.

Iris put the episode out of her mind as they walked out to the waiting family. She would think about it again later, but for now she had a job to do.

"I'm Iris," she said, shaking hands with the two adults. "I understand you're missing a dog?"

"Do you have my Petey?" the little girl asked before they could answer.

Her dad put his hands on her shoulders. "We hope so, Kyla. But if he's not here, I promise you we'll keep looking for him." He turned back to Iris. "I'm Al, and this is Linda and Kyla. We were visiting Linda's parents in Mount Vernon when the earthquake hit. Her mom fell and had to go to the hospital, and we couldn't get back here until yesterday. We had a neighbor go over to feed Petey, but the play set in the backyard knocked over the fence, and he must have gotten out. Our neighbor searched for him, and we've been looking since we got back."

"Where do you live?" Iris asked. Even though she wanted to place every single dog, she couldn't help but hope that Chert wasn't their Petey. "And can you describe your dog?"

"Our house is near Roche Harbor," Linda said. "Petey is a three-year-old border collie mix. I have some pictures of him."

Iris sighed with relief at the description. She had been thinking about the dogs she'd brought in since the quake, narrowing the options down in her mind as the family talked. Male dog—twelve. Four of them had come from the Roche Harbor area. Only one was a border collie. She knew exactly which dog belonged to them before she looked at the photos Linda showed her.

"I drew one, too," Kyla said.

She handed Iris a piece of construction paper with a drawing of three stick figures and a dog standing next to a square house with a triangle roof. Iris knelt beside her and examined the sketch.

"I have a dog here that looks like the one in your picture, Kyla. Can you wait here and I'll bring him out? I hope he's your Petey."

She got up and saw Casey watching her with an intense gaze. Chert obviously was going to remain at the shelter for the time being, and Iris felt a mixture of relief and sadness that she seemed to see reflected in Casey's expression.

"Roche Harbor Two?" Casey asked in a low voice.

Iris nodded. "Want to bring him out?"

"Sure," Casey said in a carefully casual voice. She walked toward the kennel while Iris chatted with the family and returned in a few minutes with the small border collie. As soon as he saw his people, he bounded across the parking lot with Casey running behind.

"Petey!" Kyla shouted as she and her parents hurried to meet the dog halfway. Iris felt Casey's hand rest on her shoulder as she watched the four of them huddle close, sharing tears, tail wags, and doggy licks.

"You do a good thing here, Iris," Casey whispered in her ear, making the skin on her neck shiver in response. She leaned into Casey's touch, not certain which of them needed the comfort of closeness the most. Iris loved these reunions, but they always made her realize how many other dogs were lonely and waiting for the same good luck.

And Casey must be thinking of Chert. She seemed to be enjoying her time with him, but hopefully he would soon have his own reunion. Casey would be sad when it happened, but she had to let go. She would be leaving the island once her fieldwork was done after all, and life on San Juan would go on without her.

Iris smiled at Casey and moved away from her touch. Casey wasn't the only one who had to be prepared to let go.

Chapter Eleven

Casey woke up the next morning and pulled on a pair of sweats before sleepwalking to the coffee machine. She inhaled deeply as she stretched, waiting for the coffee to finish brewing. The scent of last night's dinner lingered in the air, perfuming the room with a blend of spices Iris had rubbed on a skirt steak. Her reheating instructions had been a bit more complex for this dish, but Casey had managed to follow them, and she and Chert enjoyed a tasty meal even though the ends were a tad charred. Chert stayed close to her heels until she gave him a scoop of kibble to keep him occupied while she went to check on the pregnant cat.

She stepped over the baby gate and lay down on her stomach next to the bed. The gray cat still hid when she walked into the room, but she purred loudly whenever Casey peered at her. In the evenings, she came into the living room and perched on the counter, watching Casey and Chert from a distance. The dog didn't make any moves toward her, and the cat hadn't shown any signs of going into labor, so Casey had started to relax around them.

She hadn't realized how empty her apartment really was until she'd come to Iris's bungalow. Casey had more knick-knacks in her place, mostly rocks, and more clothes filling the closets. Signs of her work were evident on counters and tables, with rock testing kits, old seismometers, and tons of maps strewn across every surface. But the apartment was devoid of sensations. The bland smell of her frozen meals dissipated after a few minutes, and the only sound came from the television that Casey kept on most of the night even though she rarely watched it.

Everything was different here. Casey had been working so hard that she didn't need the TV to distract her and help her sleep, and she usually left it turned off. She'd lie bundled on the couch with a book, listening to the intermittent, muted barks from the kennels, Chert's snores and the cat's purrs, and the crackling of the fire. The scent of real food seeped into the house and became part of it, and the changing aromas layered together into a welcoming atmosphere. Mostly, though, Casey became hyperaware of how much she had lacked touch in her life. Chert was always near and ready for attention, and Casey loved sleeping with his warm furriness tucked close by her side. She felt other things, too—the fuzzy scratch of Iris's throw rug and the warmth of a wood fire. The pleasing achiness of muscles that had worked hard all day and the damp feeling in the air right before it started to rain.

She felt as if she had been living in a sensory-deprivation pod for the past few years. She should be overwhelmed by the assault on her senses, but instead she felt soothed by every new taste and smell.

She got dressed in several layers of clothing and took Chert with her to the kennels. Even though she had tried to tell Iris she didn't need to feed her, frozen meals appeared in her fridge every day while she was in the field. She had argued with Iris and had even offered to pay her for the dinners, but Iris just ignored her and kept stocking the refrigerator. To be honest, Casey hadn't argued too vehemently because she loved the food. Instead, she had added extra hours to her work at the shelter. The kennels were mostly repaired, and now she was working her way outward to the boundaries of the property, getting up extra early to have some daylight time to help Iris before she headed out to her faults. Her next big project would be the exercise yard, and then Iris wouldn't need her anymore.

She would be needed back at the lab, though. She had gathered some interesting data here on the island, and she had appreciated the chance to explore the crisscrossing lesser faults in person, with her view unfiltered by all but the most basic seismological equipment. The paper she was writing would be publishable, and would likely earn her some speaking opportunities at geology conferences and seminars. Altogether, a positive experience. And all too likely to end very soon.

Casey rested her hand on Chert's head as they walked. She had been so scared that the people who had arrived yesterday looking for their dog had been Chert's owners, and her response was completely unfair to him. She had to hope his people were found soon, giving him a joyful reunion like she had witnessed yesterday. He deserved nothing less, and she was selfish to want to keep him with her until she was ready to leave.

In the space of seconds, while Iris had held her hand and offered a quiet sort of support Casey had never felt before, Casey had lectured herself on thinking of the dog and not herself. Then she had done a few calculations and mapped out the remaining places she needed to explore while she was on the San Juans. She was certain her inner monologue and refocus on work had cleared her outward expression of any sign that she didn't want to lose Chert. Inside, she felt like the little girl who had been told she couldn't have a dog, but she could keep that emotion buried deep.

She stopped for a moment and concentrated on that childhood memory, but every time she thought she could grasp it, it dissolved into mental images of work and maps and problems to solve. She shook her head. Maybe it would become clearer if she didn't try so hard. She was out of practice seeking memories on purpose, but she needed to recapture this one for some reason. She had started to share it with Iris, but had lost the thread of it. Maybe she just wanted to finish telling her story.

Iris would understand. Casey knew that for a fact, especially after reading her poem. She had captured Casey's questions in a handful of words. Who was she? Why was she lonely? Why couldn't she figure out the precise formula for falling in love? Casey had been uncomfortable with the questions, and she had turned her attention to Iris and the possibility of her getting published.

Iris clearly hadn't liked that. She thought her poem was too personal to share, but she was wrong. It had felt personal to Casey, too, and other readers would likely recognize themselves in the words also. Iris had a way with them, whether writing her poem or her cards. She played with words, and they obeyed, creating humor and pathos and empathy in turn. Casey stood by her conviction that Iris should share her gift beyond the greeting cards, but Iris obviously disagreed. Casey would stash her opinion in the same place where she kept her fear of finding Chert's owners. Iris's choices were her own to make.

Casey stopped by the toolshed and got a pair of thick gloves and a handsaw. She'd start by clearing the limbs out of the exercise yard. The play area for the dogs had been hardest hit by the quake because of the trees surrounding it, but it was also a low priority for repairs. The large number of incoming animals and the kennels that housed them were higher priorities for Iris, Agatha, and Leo. They were making do for now with the smaller yard behind Iris's house, but the access to it wasn't as easy as the exercise area right next to the kennels. Casey knew she could save them time by fixing this area. And then she'd be out of projects.

Casey couldn't find the wire cutters and she turned toward the eastern end of the kennels where she thought she had heard Leo talking to the dogs. Instead, he was standing directly behind her holding the cutters. She leaped back a foot in surprise and cracked her head on the low doorway of the shed.

"Looking for these?" he asked. Casey was sort of adjusting to his uncanny ability to appear out of nowhere with something she needed, but he still caught her by surprise now and then. It would be creepy if he wasn't one of the nicest people she had ever met.

She rubbed the back of her head. "Actually, yeah, I was. Thanks, Leo."

"You're welcome. I didn't realize you'd be getting to work this early. You and Iris work too hard."

Casey didn't mind the labor, especially since she was trading it for excellent food and a comfortable place to sleep. "Has she had even an hour to herself since the earthquake?" she asked. "Every time I see her, she's doing something for the shelter or writing." Not to mention cooking the food Casey kept finding in her freezer.

Leo shook his head. "She drives herself hard. Always has, but it's been tough this week." He paused, then added, "Agatha and I will be here all day. If someone were to find a way to get

Iris off the property and, oh, out into the woods for a hike or something, Agatha and I would be very appreciative."

Casey raised her eyebrows. He was obviously talking about her, but she considered playing dumb and ignoring his meaning. She had a lot of respect for Iris and she sought out her company whenever she could, but they had a disturbing habit of rubbing each other the wrong way. Would an entire day with Iris be too abrasive? Or would they get past the initial roughness and discover a new level to their relationship? Casey liked the latter idea, but she had a feeling the first might be more likely. The options weren't worth debate, though, since Iris had been annoyed with Casey's purpose for being on the island from the start. She wouldn't want to spend the day watching Casey work.

"I doubt I could convince her to leave the shelter and go fault hunting," she said. "I think she's more interested in the animals than the terrain around here."

"Maybe you're right," Leo said. "Too bad the two of you can't find a way to compromise. You both need a break. Ah, well, I'll let you get back to the repairs. Iris brought cinnamon rolls this morning, so help yourself if you need breakfast before you get to work."

"Did she make them?" Casey had no idea how Iris was able to cook all those meals, take care of about a hundred animals, and still find time to wish everyone a Happy New Year with her cards, but she wouldn't have been surprised to hear that Iris had added *bake cinnamon rolls* to her to-do list.

Leo started walking toward the office, and Casey trailed after him, lured forward by the sweet and pungent smell of caramel and spice that grew stronger as she got closer to the source. She felt as if she'd grown a nose here on the island because she hadn't noticed scents before the way she did now.

"No," he said, holding the door open for her. "They're a specialty of one of our local bakeries. The owners just reopened, and Iris wanted to show her support."

Of course she did. Casey wasn't surprised at all. "I guess it's my civic duty to eat one, as a temporary resident of the island." She took a huge bite, closing her eyes to better savor the pastry. The dough was soft as a marshmallow, and the bottom was glazed with a deep golden syrup of caramelized sugar. Casey licked icing off her fingers and looked up to see Iris watching her from the doorway. Leo was nowhere in sight, having used his ninja skills to vanish from the room.

Iris looked flushed, but she gave Casey her usual bright smile. "Good morning. They're good rolls, aren't they?"

"Amazing," Casey agreed. Faced with Iris in the flesh, she suddenly wanted to take Leo's advice and spirit her away for the day. Her internal arguments about their incompatibility disappeared from her mind, leaving her with an aching desire just to be closer to her. Nothing about the two of them together made sense to Casey, but she was tired of listening to the logical voice inside her head. Her body was quickly overruling it.

"I'm going to Orcas Island for a few hours today," Casey said around a mouthful of cinnamon roll. "I've finished most of my work on San Juan and I wanted to see a couple of the other islands while I'm in the area since I don't know when I'll get back out here. Leo said he'd dog-sit Chert for me."

She hesitated, wondering why she felt a twinge of something—sadness?—at the thought. She'd probably get back here eventually, if only to work in the lab's substation, but she didn't know when or how long she'd stay. She liked the environment more than she'd expected and she'd felt in touch with something inside herself while she'd been here. Memories of her mother, painful and wrenching as they were, seemed more present here. But coming back and staying in a hotel wouldn't be the same. She wouldn't have Chert or her work at the shelter. Or Iris.

"Do you want to go with me?" she asked. She could see Iris mentally preparing an excuse, and she countered it before she had a chance to reject the offer. "Leo already said he and Agatha could handle the work here for the day."

"I don't know," Iris said, drawing the words out slowly. "What are you going to do on Orcas?"

"Sightsee. No earthquake studies, so you don't have to witness me rubbing my hands together and cackling with glee over the damage they cause."

Iris burst into laughter, as if she couldn't stop herself. Casey had come to love the times she could make Iris lose control like that.

"I don't think you're the wicked witch of seismology. Anymore. But I should…I shouldn't…Yes, I'll go with you."

Casey felt as surprised as Iris looked. "Well, good. I haven't checked the ferry schedule, but I think they're running more regularly than they were when I first came here. Should we leave around ten? That'll give me time to work in the exercise yard."

She was rambling. She stopped for a breath and shoved the last of her pastry in her mouth to keep herself from talking.

Iris nodded. "Okay. I'll be ready. I'll bring lunch and we can have a picnic."

"Don't go to any trouble," Casey said. "I can buy you lunch in one of the villages."

"Bread and cheese, nothing to it," Iris said. "Besides, we don't know what will be open yet. I'll meet you at the truck at ten."

Casey licked her fingers clean as she watched Iris hurry out the office door. Was she looking forward to the day, or concerned about it? They'd never spent more than a couple hours together, and they tended to argue toward the end of every conversation.

Casey picked up her tools and went out to the yard. Yes, she was looking forward to the day. Definitely.

CHAPTER TWELVE

Iris checked with Agatha before she went back to her house, to make sure she and Leo would be fine without her. After being told she was completely dispensable for the day and to get off the property before Agatha had Leo drive her off with a pitchfork, Iris turned her attention to packing a picnic lunch.

What the hell was she thinking? True, she hadn't had time to relax since the earthquake. She'd had some downtime on the ferries as she shuttled animals from other shelters to her own and once to reunite a huge Labrador with his Shaw Island owners, but she couldn't read a book or take in the scenery when she was holding leashes or crates. She could use a little time to herself to recharge.

Time to herself was the key phrase. Would time with Casey be rejuvenating or stressful?

Iris wanted to cancel, to take a few hours instead to drive around the island alone, but she knew herself too well. If she wasn't accountable to someone else, she'd just be back here before an hour was up, cleaning water dishes or exercising dogs. Maybe Agatha and Leo were right. She'd be stuck on Orcas with Casey, unable to get back until Casey drove her to the ferry. Forced time off.

Iris got a grocery bag with handles and put whatever she could find in her fridge inside. She'd just keep the conversation off her poetry and on Casey. Or the weather. Or politics. Anything less controversial to her than her poetry.

Still, despite her resolve to keep her writing separate from the day's outing, she added a blank notebook and pen to the bag. In case she found inspiration for one of her cards. Mother's Day was coming soon—according to her schedule, not the calendar—and beachy cards always were top sellers.

She realized she was humming to herself as she packed an extra sweater in the bag, and she wondered at her light mood. She supposed it was due to the lessening influx of animals that had gotten loose after the earthquake. She was beginning to see more trickle back to their owners than she was bringing in. Or maybe her mood was improved because the signs of damage were harder to spot now. The island was coming back to life as businesses reopened and families returned. Her own property reflected the awakening of the San Juans, mostly because Casey worked far too many hours cleaning and making repairs. Evidence of the disaster showed in the patchwork chain-link fences and in the huge piles of brush and branches that needed to be burned away, but those scars weren't interfering with daily life anymore. The island was healing, and Iris was as well.

Because of Casey. No matter how Iris felt about her personally—too attracted, too annoyed, too, too much—she appreciated what Casey had done for her and the shelter. It had been worth a few frozen meals and the use of the bungalow to have her there.

On her way to meet Casey, Iris stopped by the interns' house to put another dinner in the freezer and check on the gray cat. She was curled in a ball on Casey's bed, showing no signs of imminent motherhood. Iris had already asked Agatha to check on her during the day, one item in a long list of reminders, and Agatha had just rolled her eyes. Of course she and Leo would check on the cat, and give the dogs fresh water, and make sure the Twins had plenty of treats. Iris didn't need to leave them with instructions, but she wouldn't be able to enjoy her day if she hadn't given them. Best to be prepared.

"Ready to go?" Casey asked when Iris got to the lot. She was sitting in the bed of her truck, dangling her legs like a child.

Iris smiled and held up the bag. "Food and warm clothes. I'm all set."

Iris opened the passenger door, and a pile of clothes and metal cylinders threatened to fall out. Casey rushed over to help her grab the items.

"Sorry. I've been using the truck as an office." She pushed her stuff into the center of the cab, making room for Iris and her bag.

"What are these things?" Iris asked, picking up one of the gray-encased cylinders and turning it over carefully in her hands. It was heavier than it looked, solid and plain without any sign of an opening.

"Seismometers," Casey said. She brushed Iris's hands with her own as she reached over and clicked the case open using an unseen latch. The inside was as intricate as the outside was simple. "They measure shock waves, and the information shows up on a seismograph. These are simplified and portable, and I have them set up along the coast. The UW lab has more sophisticated ones throughout the Northwest."

Casey started the truck and steered them toward Friday Harbor. Iris kept her attention on the cylinder and wondered if the little machine had measured the tremor that ran through her at Casey's touch. "But the earthquake happened before you got here. What good have they done since then?"

Casey glanced over at her with a frown. "Maybe I shouldn't tell you."

"Tell me what?"

"Seismic activity happens all the time. Thousands of times a year. Most of it is too slight for people to notice. I might have missed the mainshock, but I've had a chance to witness several significant aftershocks."

Iris put the seismometer on the bench seat between her and Casey and looked out the window as they drove down the hill to the ferry dock. The town was slowly coming to life again, and she saw fewer *closed* signs on businesses. Tourists were still noticeably absent, but they would come back again.

Friday Harbor would return to normal, but would Iris? She felt betrayed somehow. Her world was supposed to be stable, but now she realized it was constantly moving and shifting below the surface. What could she count on if she couldn't even rely on the ground beneath her?

"So, you've had a successful trip to the islands? I remember how excited you were when we met on the ferry."

"And I remember how much you wanted to toss me overboard because of that excitement," Casey said as she pulled into line at the landing. Their timing was perfect, and a ferry sat at the dock waiting to be loaded with cars and pedestrians. Iris didn't remember the last time she had been able to drive directly onto a ferry without waiting for at least an hour in line. Traffic both from and to the mainland and surrounding islands was still minimal.

Iris patted the seismometer gently. "Maybe I'll settle for throwing this into the Sound. Let's see how the day goes."

Casey laughed and put the truck in park. They were only five cars from the bow, and Iris saw gray water churning as the ferry's motor kept it pressed against the dock. They got out and walked up the stairwell and onto the observation deck.

"Have you learned anything new while you've been here?" Iris asked once they were leaning on the wooden railing and facing away from Friday Harbor. She had to raise her voice to be heard over the motor as the ferry began its slow push away from the shore. "I promise not to dump you in the sea if you talk about your work."

"Okay, I'll tell you about it," Casey said, wrapping her forearms around the railing in an exaggerated grip. "I'm new at the lab, and I'm pretty sure I was sent here to be tested. The UW has measuring instruments all around Puget Sound. Serious shit that makes the seismometer you saw in the truck look medieval in comparison. The data is relayed to the lab and analyzed by computers and a whole building full of scientists."

"So, what good…um…?"

"What good am I doing here?"

Iris grinned at Casey's self-deprecating tone. "I was trying to find a nicer way to ask the question."

"Yeah, I could tell. Thanks."

Iris bumped Casey with her shoulder, just hard enough to make her loosen her grip on the railing a little. "So, why did they send you here?"

"Sometimes a pair of human eyes can see more than the most sophisticated instruments in the world," Casey said, looking toward the approaching Orcas Island. "I guess my boss wants to find out what I'll observe while I'm here."

Iris had no doubt Casey's eyes saw more than most people's. Sometimes, around the shelter, Iris would turn around and catch Casey watching her with an intensity that seemed to reach to Iris's core. She was torn between wanting Casey to know and see her even more clearly and wanting to run and hide.

"And what have your human eyes seen when you've gone traipsing through the woods?"

"Well, I've found evidence of displacement in quite a few areas, and that can help us map the minor faults on the island. We know where some of them are and we can guess at others using LIDAR mapping and geologic profiles, but I've been able to observe changes that likely occurred in response to the initial rupture."

Casey had seemed reluctant to talk much about her work, probably because she was worried they might have a repeat of the argument from their first ferry ride, but once she got started, her passion took over and she spoke rapidly, gesturing with her hands as she explained low angle thrust faults and wave propagation.

Iris no longer resented Casey for her ability to discuss the earthquake with such obvious fascination. She had seen her around Chert and the other animals enough to recognize Casey's kind heart and caring nature. The coldness she had presumed when they first met seemed to be more due to self-protection—from what, Iris didn't know—than uncaring detachment.

Now she followed Casey's words with a mixture of interest and anxiety. She recognized what comfort someone could have if they understood why the ground shook, and she appreciated Casey's enthusiasm for her work, but she couldn't separate her experience during the earthquake from any discussion about the mechanics of it.

"Will any of your observations help you learn how to predict earthquakes?" Iris asked during a pause in Casey's geology class.

"That's always the goal," Casey said. "What I've learned here will help us understand rupture propagation a little better." She turned her back to the railing and leaned her elbows on it, tilting her face toward the sky.

With Casey's attention on the gulls and clouds scooting overhead, Iris gave herself the rare permission to observe her without restraint. Her body was slender and strong, and the way she was standing gave her shape and curve even in her bulky red sweatshirt. The wind ruffled her short hair, and Casey swiped at it with a gesture that had become familiar to Iris. She let Casey's words blend into the background sounds of the slurp and splash of waves against the ferry as she imagined running her fingers through Casey's hair and down her neck, tracing the outline of her small, beautiful breasts and her tight stomach.

Iris realized Casey had stopped talking, but Iris's imaginary hands were still moving lower. She closed her eyes for a moment and opened them again to find Casey watching her.

"What?" Iris asked. "I didn't catch that."

"What part did you miss?" Casey's voice sounded rougher than normal, as if she understood that Iris hadn't missed a single part of her body even though she hadn't heard many of her words.

The ferry's horn signaled their arrival at Orcas, and Iris gladly pushed away from the railing and started walking back to the truck. "Most of it," Iris admitted over her shoulder as they walked down the stairs. She wasn't about to admit *why* she hadn't been listening.

"I just said that once we have faults mapped out and learn how they affect each other, we'll be better able to predict where earthquakes will happen and how the damage will extend from the hypocenter."

Iris wove through the tightly packed cars. "Is this break-through going to happen soon?"

"When you say *soon*, are you talking in geologic time? If so, yes."

"How about in normal human time?" Iris got in the truck and put on her seat belt.

"Not so much. But we're trying."

"You're a dreamer," Iris said as they eased their way off the ferry and past the handful of buildings making up Orcas Landing. An inn and restaurant—both closed for the season, not because of the earthquake—a square ferry terminal, and a convenience store, each painted white with a rust-colored roof. Unlike Friday Harbor, where tourists were dropped right into the lap of the largest town, Orcas Island hid its more populated villages from first glance. Iris had always noticed the dichotomy on this island, where the population seemed torn between a de-sire to welcome paying visitors to its quaint shops, galleries, and inns and a more pressing hope that everyone would just leave them alone to enjoy their beautiful and remote island in peace.

"I'm more practical than you," Iris continued. "So let me know when your fantasies come true and your seismo-thingies can do more than measure earthquakes as they happen. Or when you find a mythical unicorn that can predict the future using the glitter on its horn."

Iris smiled as she watched the tree-lined road slip past as they headed deeper onto the U-shaped island from the landing at the tip of the northern arm. She assumed they were going to Eastsound, the largest village that was situated on the inner elbow of the island. Maybe they could skip her hastily prepared picnic lunch and eat at the wonderful seafood restaurant at the marina. And she could show Casey through her favorite art gallery, where the specialty was blown glass in a variety of colors and patterns. And she could browse in the bookstore and find…

Casey turned left on Deer Harbor Road instead of continuing toward the top of the U and Eastsound. "You're the artistic one, not me. I'm scientific. Logical. I understand that we need to study the earth systematically for years before we can learn everything we need to know. No relying on unicorns or leprechauns. Just hard facts and miles of data."

"Please," Iris said with a snort. "I thought you were nothing but cold logic when we met, but I realized I was wrong when I saw you get all mushy about Chert."

"I do *not* get mushy about anything. Except maybe a strikingly beautiful granite outcropping, but who doesn't? If anyone is sentimental in this truck, it's the poet sitting next to me."

"I write seasonal greeting cards for money. I'm like an assembly line, churning out holiday sayings like clockwork. I've always been practical," Iris repeated. The conversation had begun as a playful one, but she was starting to feel uncomfortable. She wished she was more spontaneous and brilliant, like Casey was. Why was she fighting so hard to be defined as efficient and unimaginative, even though she knew it was true? She was the type to call ahead for reservations no matter where she went. The kind who filled her freezer with meals prepared just in case. Of course, they had come in handy this week, but usually she just ended up inviting Agatha and Leo over to help her finish them off.

Iris decided to drop the conversation, and she was relieved that Casey didn't seem interested in pursuing it further, either. They were silent until Casey pulled into a parking spot near the West Sound marina.

"Come on, I want to show you something."

Iris looked through her window at the gray, cold outdoors. "What? Can I see it from inside here, where it's warm?"

Casey came around the truck and opened the passenger door, grabbing Iris's hand and pulling her out. "I doubt it. I'm not even sure what I'm looking for, but I'll know it when I see it."

"Reassuring," Iris muttered. She zipped her jacket up to her throat, but as soon as they began walking she noticed it wasn't as cold as it had been on the ferry, where the winds had seeped through her clothes and chilled the skin underneath. Casey kept her hand for a few moments, and the contact with her was more likely responsible for Iris's sudden warmth than the sheltered location of the small harbor village.

"When there aren't this many clouds, you can see a lovely view of Mount Baker from here," Iris said, gesturing toward the east. To the south, across the eastern edge of a small bay, she could see the distant ferry that had brought them here departing from Orcas Landing.

Casey laughed, giving Iris's hand a squeeze before she let it go. "Typical Washington State tour guide," she said. She mimicked the lilting voice of a tour operator. *"If it weren't so cloudy, you'd have a spectacular view of Mount Rainier. If it weren't raining, Mount St. Helens would be visible to the south.* Do these places really exist, or do the locals just make them up?"

Iris played along, although she knew Casey had scaled her share of mountains searching for fault lines and interesting rocks along the Pacific Crest Trail, and that she knew exactly how real they were. "Shh. We're not supposed to talk about this with non-locals, but if work dries up in the greeting card business, I'm going to take a job as an illustrator for travel brochures. You can make a fortune if you come up with catchy new mountain names for each one you draw."

Casey laughed. "And if people come here and want to climb one of these fake mountains, you can earn extra cash painting *Closed because of avalanche* signs. Oh, look!"

She jogged over to a shelf of gray-green rock, and Iris followed behind, her tennis shoes sliding over the smooth and rounded stones making up the shoreline. She slipped once, bracing her hand against the polished trunk of a tree that had been weathered to the soft gray of driftwood. Once she had her balance again, she caught up to Casey and stood beside her, trying to figure out what she found so absorbing. As far as Iris could tell, nothing interesting was on top of the tilted, rectangular rock. She squinted and looked closer, expecting an ancient cave painting or rare fossil to appear. But it was just a rock.

"Don't tell me this is your idea of sightseeing," Iris said, mentally comparing this to the day she had envisioned at the Eastsound village. "It's just a rock, and not a very pretty one at that."

Casey turned toward Iris and held up both hands as if to ward off her words. "I am going to pretend I didn't hear what you just said." She picked up a small chunk of black-and-white speckled rock with undertones of the same olive drab color of the larger one, and handed it to Iris. Iris hefted it in her hand, still unimpressed by the coarse-grained rock.

"This is diorite. A lot of the rocks on Orcas are from the Devonian to Permian eras, from two hundred fifty to about four hundred million years ago. But below them is a layer called the Turtleback Basement Complex, and parts of it are exposed because of erosion of the younger rocks. You're likely holding something in your hand that is over five hundred forty million years old."

Casey put her hand over Iris's and tilted it until Iris could see the crystalline facets of the rock glint in the diffused sunlight. Casey watched the movement with a reverence that was almost palpable to Iris. "When magma cools slowly, deep in the earth, it forms igneous rocks with large crystals like this one has. These rocks are ancient, Iris. They've been hidden for millions of years, waiting for the relentless waves and wind and rain to erode the blanket of stone above them and expose them to view. They hold all the secrets to the earth's past and future. If we can be as silent and patient as they are, we can see what they're trying to tell us and read the story of our world in their shape, composition, and placement."

Casey let go of Iris's hand again, and Iris nearly dropped the small rock as she felt jolted back to reality by the absence of Casey's touch. Instead, she put it in the pocket of her jeans and felt its sharp edges press against her inner thigh, pushing against her with the residual sensation of Casey's fingers.

"See?" Iris said. "You're the one who should be a poet. The only thing I could do with rocks is make terrible puns for greeting cards, like *Thank you for being so gneiss*, or *Happy birthday to someone who grows boulder every year*. Shale I go on?"

Casey laughed and jabbed Iris playfully with her elbow. "Stop, or I'll diorite now."

Iris joined in her laughter, wondering when she had ever felt inclined to be goofy and silly with someone like she did with Casey. From the start, Casey had been able to draw smiles and lightness out of Iris. Those tendencies must always have been there because they felt as natural to Iris as breathing or packing freezers with food, but she had needed a catalyst like Casey to pull them from her.

Iris looked at the rectangular formation again, with a different sort of understanding, and she watched it transform from a clump of nondescript rock into something entirely new. Casey had been slowly eroding Iris's protective shell since she came to the islands, using her unique and wonderful blend of science and something approaching prayer, of a deep respect for the past and a joyous hope for what sorts of understanding the future might bring. Iris was the present, embedded in the here-and-now because she was afraid to be disappointed by her hope for more or paralyzed by her regrets from the past.

She backed up until her legs bumped against the large hunk of driftwood and she pulled herself up so she was sitting on it with her feet dangling a few inches from the ground. She took her notepad and pen out of the large grocery bag and held the bag toward Casey, never taking her eyes off the rock because she didn't want the words forming in her mind to sink below the surface again.

"Food. And a blanket," she said. Casey hurried over and took the bag from her, luckily not saying a word to break the spell. Iris uncapped her pen and started to write.

And didn't stop until lines had drained out of her and onto the page, arranged and rearranged until they were where they belonged. She looked around—startled by reality for a moment—and saw Casey watching her from the ledge of rocks that separated the parking area from the lower sea level. She was wedged between two large boulders, partly sitting on the blanket and partly wrapped in it.

"You must be freezing," Iris said, wondering how long she had been writing. She never could tell if it had been minutes or hours until she looked at a clock. "I'm sorry I kept you here for…how long has it been?"

"Only an hour and a half," Casey said. "And don't be sorry. I loved watching you being so intense and focused on creating. It reminded me of—"

She stopped and looked away, her face flushing slightly as if she was embarrassed or surprised that she had been about to admit something to Iris. Iris understood, though. When she wrote like this, she sometimes felt like she was casting a spell. The world grew more intimate and boundaries were lowered. Casey must have been drawn into the feeling after watching Iris in silence for so long.

"What?" she prompted. "What did you remember?"

"My mom. She liked to play the piano, and she'd get the same faraway expression on her face like you had. Not distant, but like the world was expanding into something larger and more magical than it normally was."

Iris turned to a new page and wrote Casey's words on it. "I'm going to keep notes of things you say. Someday I'll show them to you and prove that you're the one who should be the poet."

"Will you let me read what you just wrote?" Casey asked, with a tentative note in her voice. She seemed to understand what a personal request she was making, and she gave Iris space to say no.

"On one condition," Iris said. A question had come to her while she was writing, and she wanted to know the answer. "If I can ask you some things about your childhood."

Casey shrugged, giving the impression that sharing the details of her life was no big deal to her, but Iris felt the currents of stress beneath Casey's casual gesture. "Sure. Go ahead."

She got up and handed Iris a wedge of crusty rye bread, slathered with a thick layer of cream cheese and topped with a few slivers of coral-colored smoked salmon. "Eat first, though. You must be starving after writing so furiously."

Her hand brushed against Casey's as she took the open-faced sandwich from her, and they seemed to linger together for a few seconds beyond what was necessary. Iris took a huge bite of food, telling herself it was only the tanginess of cream cheese that was making her mouth water.

"You're obviously fascinated with the earth's past," Iris said, picking a piece of the salmon off her bread and eating it separately, letting the flavors of sea and smoke permeate her mouth, like the memory of a late-night bonfire on the beach. "But you seem more reluctant to talk about your own. What was it like? Were you happy?"

"Happy. Hmm." Casey bent her knees and hugged them close. "I suppose. I went to great schools and had opportunities most kids aren't given. If I ever wanted a book or chemistry lab set or anything, my father and grandparents got it for me."

"But no dog." Iris didn't wait for an answer. Casey had already told her about the no-pets rule. "What were you like as a child?"

"Very well-behaved," Casey said with an impish grin. "I saved all my rebellion for college and graduate school. I admittedly went a little wild during those years, but never at the expense of my grades. Controlled rebellion, I suppose."

"Was everyone in your family a scientist?" Iris felt like she was interrogating Casey, but she was prepared to keep asking questions until Casey's story started to flow on its own, without prompting. Then Iris might learn something to help her understand Casey better.

"My dad is a psychiatrist. Not the kind who sees patients, but more of a researcher with drug companies. Antidepressants and all that. I sometimes wondered if I was such a good child because he was mashing up some experimental meds in my applesauce." Casey laughed sharply and waved her hand. "Don't look so shocked. I'm kidding. I was just as well-mannered when I was with my mom, and she'd never have done that. Of course, if I hadn't been so good, he might have been tempted."

Iris laughed along with Casey, but she felt saddened by what she said. Not because she really thought Casey's father had drugged her—she was obviously joking about it—but because she seemed to have been the type of child who wanted to please people and felt she had to behave well or else approval would have vanished.

"My grandparents were both neurobiologists. They met in a research lab and worked together for years, until they retired. They were always together."

"And your mom?"

Casey frowned. "She was a teacher, but I'm not really sure what kind. I've always guessed she would have been great with younger kids, in elementary school, but I don't know for certain. No one talked about her much." Casey sighed and drew her knees even closer. "I understand why, as an adult. My dad was out of the picture before I was born, so he'd had no experience raising a child when I arrived. My grandparents were busy with work and weren't prepared for me, either. Suddenly I arrived, not just an unexpected four-year-old child to take care of, but a grieving one. They wanted to make me feel better, and they did it by helping me find ways to deal with sadness by focusing on other things. They barely mentioned her, and they'd distract me with questions or mathematical problems to solve if I brought her up. I guess I got pretty good at refocusing, because I can usually turn off memories like flicking off a light switch."

Casey paused and stared out toward the bay while Iris fumed inside. She was glad to hear that Casey's dad wasn't seeing patients and giving them the advice he had given his own child. She hated that Casey hadn't been allowed to remember her mother.

"It's different here," Casey finally said, "with Chert and the shelter animals, and with the people I've met here. With you. Memories of my mom seem closer. Maybe it's because I'm having to slow my usual pace to match island time. Or maybe it's because cooking and pets and hiking in the woods provide triggers that bring her to mind." She added her next sentences in a quieter voice, as if admitting to a dark secret. "I tried to push the memories away at first, but I don't anymore. I want more of them. I wish I hadn't forgotten so much."

She grew silent, and Iris decided to stop asking questions and give Casey a break. She stood up and handed the notebook to Casey before stopping to pack the remains of their lunch back into the bag.

"Why don't I drive us back to the ferry landing so you can read my poem."

Casey got up and wrapped her blanket covered arms around the notepad. "Thank you," she said. She put her arm across Iris's shoulders as they walked to the truck, sharing the warmth of the blanket and her body as she curved close.

CHAPTER THIRTEEN

Casey read Iris's poem slowly as they drove back to the ferry landing. Once Iris had maneuvered the pickup on board, Casey read the poem again. Neither of them seemed to have any interest in standing on the observation deck in the cold again for the short trip back to Friday Harbor, so they remained inside the warm cab.

Iris leaned against the driver's side door with her head resting on the window and her eyes looking forward, toward home. Casey struggled to find the right words to explain how she felt about Iris's poem, and she reread it again silently to give herself time to think.

Iris had listened to her talk about the Turtleback Complex with the indulgent expression people usually offered to children who prattled on about nothing in particular, and she hadn't seemed to grasp the importance of what Casey was trying to express. But Iris *had* understood Casey, in a way she hadn't experienced before. Reading Iris's poem was like hearing herself talk—inside her head, where the meaning and the words were connected in a way they rarely were when spoken out loud. She felt as if the poem had been written for and about her alone, but she guessed that it was personal for Iris as well.

"I think I've come up with the definition of a truly great poet," Casey said, speaking quietly in the enclosed space. The sky was already growing dark, as the early winter sunset and the heavy cloud cover teamed up to give Casey the feeling that she and Iris were all alone in the world.

Iris shifted until her back and shoulders were against the door and she was facing Casey. "What's your definition?"

"A great poet somehow hears the conversations you have inside your head, and then writes them down using the exact right words, so you understand perfectly what you were trying to say to yourself. I know how much I love those ancient rocks, and I thought I knew why, but you explained me better than I could ever do myself."

Iris smiled. "I'm glad you like the poem. It's yours if you want it."

Casey appreciated how easily Iris was able to give a part of herself away, but she suspected it was as much because Iris didn't understand the true worth of her creation as it was because she was exceptionally generous. The cab was too cozy, and she was too comfortable being this close to Iris to risk putting distance between them by bringing up publishing again, so Casey held herself back from offering Iris more encouragement to sell her poems. "Thank you. I love it," she said instead.

She closed her eyes and rested in the quiet. The truck rocked slightly as waves broke against the side of the ferry. The smell of damp dog—Chert loved to go swimming every chance he got—and sea air filled the cab. Casey hadn't realized salt water had such a distinctive aroma, but the two scents followed her everywhere these days and had come to mean something to her.

Home? No. Chert had a home of his own somewhere, and Casey's was deep within the city. Exhaust fumes and the Indian takeout place just below her apartment smelled like home.

Now Iris's fragrance was added to the mix of this new scent. Honey and spices and something floral—lavender?—were permeating the seat where Iris's hair and skin touched it and floating through the air. How long would Casey be back in the city before the last hints of ocean and dog and Iris disappeared?

Casey opened her eyes and sat up abruptly, relieved to see the lights of Friday Harbor only a few yards away. She would miss Iris. Damn it, she'd miss the whole island. Maybe she was only feeling this sense of premature nostalgia because she had taken too few vacations over the years. Maybe all she needed was more time away. Then she'd see that other kinds of places had interesting things to do and see. Other cities had beautiful women and animals. She should get out of the lab and go horseback riding in the mountains or dancing with artists in the desert. Whatever it took to prove to herself that San Juan wasn't the only beautiful vacation spot in the world. Chert wasn't the only animal. And Iris wasn't the only woman.

She was the only woman in the truck, though, and she filled Casey's senses almost to the point of oversaturation. Casey had been amazed by the sudden influx of scent and taste into her life that now seemed bland in comparison. Iris surprised her in the same way. Every other woman Casey had dated and kissed seemed flat to her now. They didn't have the taste, smell, or texture that Iris offered.

Casey's first reaction, as usual when she felt overwhelmed, was to bolt. Get far away from this tiny and remote island and everything associated with it. But she would be leaving soon, going back to her apartment and her job. Would a few nights of indulgence be disastrous, or would they satisfy her senses enough to let her return to her old world sated and happy?

She'd start small.

"My friend Jazz just reopened her pub," she said. "I'd love to go there and support her. Would you like to come with me and get some dinner before we head back to the shelter? It should be a quiet night there, with so few tourists in town."

"I love her cooking," Iris said. She seemed to be wrestling with the idea of prolonging their day, and Casey gave her time to decide.

"I'll call Agatha and Leo. If everything is going well at the shelter, I'd like to get a quick dinner."

They switched seats so Casey could drive off the ferry while Iris called home. Casey listened as she asked about the gray cat and the Twins and Chert, pausing in between as Agatha apparently gave her detailed updates on each one. She parked near the pub, figuring Jazz would be long closed by the time Iris asked about each individual animal. Luckily, she grouped some of them together and saved time.

"All the animals are okay?" Casey asked, just to be polite because she figured Agatha or Leo would have called them earlier if anything had gone wrong. She admired how dedicated Iris was to the shelter, but Casey didn't have the same attachment to the animals.

"Yes, they're doing well," Iris said. "I'm starving. Lunch was too small."

She got out of the truck, and Casey followed. "So Agatha and Leo didn't have trouble taking care of everything alone today?"

"No, they're fine. Jazz sometimes makes an incredible pot roast as one of her weekly specials. I wonder if she'll have it on the menu tonight?" Iris walked toward the front door of the pub. Casey had been there to see Jazz and share meals with her, but she was used to entering through the back door and eating in the kitchen. She veered back onto the sidewalk and hurried to catch up to Iris.

"So, how's Chert?" she finally gave in and asked. She had been hoping Iris would volunteer the information, but she hadn't, and Casey had to give up her façade of indifference and come right out and ask.

Iris held the door open for Casey and grinned at her, as if she had known all along how much Casey wanted to hear about him.

"He's good, you old softie. Agatha said he's been following Leo around all day, but he keeps going back to the bungalow and looking for you."

"Really?" Casey was at a loss for words. Did he really miss her, or was Iris just making that up? She had loved being alone with Iris, but she hadn't gone this long without Chert at her side since she found him in the woods. She missed him.

"Yes, really. He'll be there waiting for you when we get back home." Iris patted her on the shoulder, and then walked into the bar and directly over to hug Jazz. Casey followed more slowly, staring in surprise at the crowds of people filling the small space. The pub was decorated in a typical fashion meant to simulate a British pub experience, with mirrored signs on the walls advertising Newcastle and Guinness and dartboards hanging uncomfortably close to tables where diners would sit. Nearly every seat was taken, and the noise level seemed to indicate that everyone knew everyone else and they were all participating in a very loud group conversation.

Jazz let go of Iris and captured Casey in one of her gripping bear hugs. "Good to see you two," she yelled over the steady din. She elbowed Casey in the ribs. "Together, that is. Iris, I've been meaning to thank you for...well, you know."

Iris just shrugged and smiled. "Any chance you're serving your pot roast tonight?"

"Of course! Just the thing for a cold, cloudy day. Same for you, Casey?" She looked behind them. "Didn't you bring your dog? Chert—have you ever heard such a name?" She aimed the last sentence in Iris's direction with a shake of her head.

"He's back at the shelter with Leo," Casey said. "And fish and chips for me, please. Is there an open table?"

"A little one in the back, just the thing. Nice and private." Jazz waved in the general direction of what looked like a wall of people. Casey didn't know how any part of the pub could be considered private. "Have a seat and I'll bring your beer right over."

They slowly worked their way through the crowd. Everyone seemed to know Iris, and Casey noticed that most of them gave her a hug and thanked her for something. No one specified exactly what she had done, but she seemed to be a popular fixture in the community, just as Casey would have expected. She had seen Iris working at the shelter and on her cards, and she wondered when she found the time to do more.

They finally reached a tiny empty table that was wedged between two high bars that patrons were using as resting places for their drinks while they played pool. Obviously most of the people were locals. Casey wondered if they ate in a different place every night, just to help the business owners recoup some of their losses. She wouldn't be surprised if they had few meals at home until the tourist trade resumed.

Casey leaned close so she could talk to Iris without shouting. "Why is everyone saying thank you?"

Iris shrugged and Casey was near enough to feel the movement. She scooched her chair even closer. "It's just a polite thing to say," Iris said.

"Yes, when someone does something for you. What have you been up to?"

"Nothing much. Probably a lot less than most others are doing. A frozen meal here, a few dollars there. We've all had to pull together."

Casey nodded, as if Iris's statement was something she experienced all the time, but it had been a foreign concept to her until she came here. Not that she wouldn't have stopped to help anyone who needed her after the earthquake—plenty of passengers had needed her in the immediate aftermath of the event, but that was just what everyone did in an emergency. She had never been close enough to neighbors to even know their names, let alone band together with them to survive a crisis.

Would she be a different person in a town like this? Would she be part of this community like Iris was, or would she keep herself at a distance even here? Iris seemed to be successful with her writing, enough to support herself and her shelter, but Casey doubted she had a fortune hidden away somewhere. She had been hit hard by the earthquake, with all the extra mouths to feed. Still, she had thought about her neighbors and friends, and had apparently been sharing what she had with them. Her humble explanation for the thanks she had been receiving didn't match up to the effusiveness of the people thanking her.

Casey leaned over and gave Iris a kiss on the cheek. "You're amazing," she said. Iris looked surprised by the gesture, but Jazz—who had just arrived with their mugs of pale gold liquid—was beaming in her usual *I told you so* way.

"Here you go. Your food will be out soon, but if you get hungry you can just nibble on each other until I get back."

She walked away, laughing loudly at her own joke, before Casey could formulate a response. Iris's skin blushed to a deep shade of pink, but she stayed close, with her shoulder just touching Casey's. Casey took a sip of her ale to hide her own embarrassed response.

"Jazz is just…" Iris started but paused, as if searching for the correct defining word.

"I know," Casey said. Indefinable.

"So, I told you all my childhood secrets today," she said. "What was yours like? I'm picturing you growing up in a huge house full of dogs and cats and frogs and guinea pigs. With lots of brothers and sisters."

Iris visibly winced, and Casey set her mug on the table and covered Iris's hand with hers. "Oh, I'm sorry. Did I say something wrong?"

Iris shook her head. "Not at all. I mean, yes, you're wrong about my childhood, but no, you didn't say anything hurtful."

Casey had obviously struck a nerve, but she stayed silent and let Iris choose how to explain it to her.

"You were right about the house, though," Iris said. The loud room forced them to be close, and Casey could smell the crisp hints of apple and hops from the ale on Iris's breath. She briefly lost the thread of Iris's words as she imagined kissing her and tasting the ale's flavors mixed with the honey and vanilla sweetness of Iris herself. She shook herself mentally, like Chert after a swim in the cold sea water, and brought her attention back to Iris's story.

"…huge, and full of rooms my parents wanted to fill with children. They were both from enormous families—I have thirty-nine cousins and even I lose track of my own family when I start factoring in more distant relatives. But my parents could only have me."

"They must have doted on you," Casey said, but she was only saying the words because she fervently hoped they were true. Something in Iris's expression told her otherwise. Her face was smooth, lacking the tiny lines and curves that came when she smiled or laughed or frowned. She looked younger without those lines that came from experience and engagement with the world around her. Vulnerable.

"They did, in a way." Iris fiddled with a packet of sugar from the container on the table, folding the edges in toward each other. "They had tried to have children for years before I came along, so they were quite a bit older than my friends' parents. They were very protective of me, like I was something to be cherished, and I had a lot of rules to follow. At the same time, though, I always knew I wasn't enough. They tried for more children, and every disappointment seemed to destroy something inside them a little more. I was never enough to make them feel whole."

Jazz stopped by and set their food on the table with a wink, and both Casey and Iris thanked her with smiles that didn't even hint at the serious conversation they were having.

As soon as she was gone, Casey reached for the bottle of malt vinegar. She was sure Iris was exaggerating about her parents' disappointment in only having her. She must have heard something out of context when she was too young to understand it fully. How could any parent not be happy with a loving and kind child like Iris must have been? She thought briefly of her own persistent attempts to make her dad and grandparents proud of her, but she pushed her memories away.

"How could you not be enough for anyone? Just because they wanted more kids doesn't mean they didn't love you." Casey sprinkled vinegar on her fish, and as soon as the drops hit the hot, fried batter they infused the air with an explosion of malt and tang.

Iris blinked. "Will the one bottle be enough for you? I can get another from the table over there."

Casey laughed, glad to see Iris's humor make an appearance. "I'll let you know if I need more, thanks. Usually one bottle is enough."

"To what, destroy your taste buds?"

"Ha-ha." She held the bottle out and tipped it threateningly over Iris's plate of gravy-covered meat and vegetables. "Want some? It'll add a nice tartness to your food."

"Back off," Iris said, laughing and brandishing her fork.

Casey put the bottle back in its place and ate one of Jazz's homemade fries. She was torn between wanting to hear more of Iris's life story and wanting to ease off and let Iris enjoy her meal.

Iris seemed to intuit Casey's curiosity because she resumed her story. "This wasn't a one-time conversation I overheard, Casey. This was the theme of my childhood, especially after we spent any time with one of my aunts or uncles and their huge families. Looking back, I can't remember my parents spending time together or having much of a relationship. They seemed to be together because they both had a desire for more kids. They lived in the past, with the losses and miscarriages, and they hoped for a future with more children. We didn't live in the present like my friends did, with vacations and game nights and family time."

And now Iris filled the empty bungalow with interns, pregnant cats, and Casey. And she wouldn't allow herself to hope for things in the future, like published poems. "So, you've learned how to live in the present because of them," Casey said. "That's a great attitude to have in life. Seize the day, and all that."

Iris gave a humorless laugh that didn't disrupt the smoothness of her forehead and cheeks. "I guess. I'm just not brave enough to do much seizing. I take the easy way out."

Casey shook her head. "What's easy about your life? There's plenty of good in it, but you're one of the hardest working and most caring people I've ever met. I don't see how moving to the island, running a shelter, and being part of this community is taking an easy way out."

Iris bumped her shoulder. "You're very nice," she said in an *I don't really believe what you're saying, but it's a nice sentiment* kind of way. "Speaking of enjoying the present, you have to try this pot roast."

Casey didn't fight Iris's attempt to end the conversation about her childhood. She did her part to keep the mood lighter for the rest of their meal, tasting Iris's dinner and trying to wrestle the plate away from her—partly to keep Iris laughing and playful, but also because the food was melt-in-your-mouth delicious and she wanted more. She settled for trading a piece of fish and a handful of fries for half of Iris's remaining pot roast.

After a prolonged battle with Jazz over the bill—she refused to accept money from them, and Iris had to distract her while Casey paid the bartender—they finally made it outside. Iris started toward the truck, but Casey took her hand and held her back.

"How about a short walk?" she asked. The night was cool, but not windy or rainy. Casey had spent a lot of the day with the thought that she'd be leaving soon in the back of her mind. Probably the last ferry ride until she took it back to Seattle. Probably the last time she'd eat at Jazz's pub. She wanted to prolong the day she had spent with Iris because she wasn't ready to leave her just yet.

"Sure," Iris said. She slipped her arm around Casey's waist as if they walked closely together all the time, and it felt just as natural for Casey to reach around and hold Iris tightly against her.

They walked toward the landing in a comfortable silence. A few cars passed them, and most of the businesses were still open. When they got to the bottom of the hill, Casey saw that the Thai fusion restaurant she had been hoping to try when she first arrived was nearly as full as Jazz's pub had been. She remembered how hesitant she'd been then about staying on the island with none of the distractions of Seattle at her disposal.

She was different now. She slept better and ate better— thanks to Iris and Jazz. She could spend entire evenings reading and chatting with Chert and the elusive cat. Far from the boredom she had anticipated, she felt fuller here. Like life was richer, and all her senses were more in tune with it.

Right now, the sense of touch overrode everything else. Iris's hands were a little rough from the work she did, and Casey had never before appreciated how much more wonderful they were than hands kept smooth with expensive lotions and little manual labor. When Iris touched her, she fired up Casey's nerve endings. Even where their skin wasn't in contact, Casey felt Iris's every move. Her jacket scratched against Casey's sweatshirt with a brushing motion that wasn't tentative or partial. And when their thighs occasionally nudged each other, with denim rasping against denim, Casey thought she was going to lose control.

She pulled Iris into the dark alcove of a closed real estate office and stood facing her, their mouths close enough for their breath to intermingle. "You are enough, Iris. More than enough. Don't let anyone convince you that you aren't."

Iris smiled, and the skin at her temples crinkled in the way Casey loved to see. She reached up a hand and brushed Casey's bangs out of her eyes, mirroring the gesture Casey knew she herself made all the time. The pads of Iris's fingers trailed over Casey's cheekbones and rubbed across her lips. Iris watched the movement of her hand, and Casey felt her gaze with as much intensity as she felt the gentle pressure from Iris's fingers. There was a heaviness in her chest and she realized she was holding her breath. She exhaled, and Iris closed the distance between them and kissed Casey's open mouth.

She had thought Iris's fingers had felt good when they touched her, but they didn't compare to Iris's lips. They moved over Casey's mouth with a confidence Casey hadn't expected from Iris, but one she understood. This wasn't the kind of confidence that came from tons of experience and skill—rather, it flowed into a kiss between two women who fit together naturally. Casey felt her world shifting as their kiss deepened, as if their mouths were two sides of a fault plane and the friction between them was causing a level of seismic activity Casey had never experienced before.

She pulled back from the kiss and rested her forehead against Iris's. She'd keep the geology metaphors to herself, but neither of them could deny what was building between them, however they chose to describe it.

"I'm not here for much longer," she said.

"I know." Iris's answer was little more than a whisper.

"We can stop now, or we can live in the present. Spend what time we have together."

Iris hesitated. Casey didn't want to push her beyond what she was ready for. She talked about living for now, but she also said she wanted to play it safe. What Casey was offering was only for the moment, and it definitely didn't feel safe for her heart. But she was willing to risk it. Was Iris? She wasn't anything Iris would want long-term. She didn't belong here, in this community. She wasn't the animal expert Iris was. She was a scientist, not a poet. She wasn't sure if Iris would be willing to compromise so much for what promised to be an amazing handful of nights.

"We can think of it like a vacation fling," Casey said, trying to keep her tone light and carefree. Did she need to prove she wasn't completely invested in this connection between them to Iris, or to herself? "You know, a time when you do things you normally wouldn't do."

"Like me?" Iris pulled away. Her voice held a harshness that made the soft, sensual closeness between them disappear. "So when you said I was enough, you meant for right now. I'm enough for a night of sex, but nothing more?"

"Whoa, that is not what I meant," Casey said, her own tone sounding louder and angrier than she liked. "I just meant we wouldn't be together otherwise. We're very different, and we live in different places—"

"What is it exactly, Casey? I'm not sophisticated enough for a city girl like you? I'm not daring enough for your scientific expeditions?"

Casey hesitated in stunned silence. How could Iris think she was the one who was inadequate? Casey had been thinking the same thing about herself. She wasn't stable, connected. She didn't welcome people and animals into her life with open arms like Iris did. By the time she was ready to form words, Iris was on her way back to the truck, and Casey had no choice but to follow. They drove in a tense silence, broken twice as Casey tried to explain herself but was shut down by Iris. Finally, she gave up and concentrated on getting them back to the shelter, where they went their separate ways.

Chapter Fourteen

Iris spent the next morning hidden away in her home office until she saw Casey's pickup leave the shelter's parking lot. She felt a little cowardly, but she really did have a ton of paperwork to do. The work in the kennels and in the cats' area was only one part of the rescue work she performed. A lot of what she did each day was more administrative. She read through a dozen emails asking about lost pets and possible adoptions, and answered each of them. She updated photos on the shelter's website and social media sites, adding new anecdotes where she could. She did everything in her power to make a connection between a potential forever home and an animal. The correlation was direct—the more personal stories she added, the higher her adoption rate, so she tried not to resent the amount of time she had to spend with her computer instead of her animals.

Today, however, she was actively searching for more busy-work to keep her inside. She had spent a restless night, alternately railing internally at Casey and wanting to sneak through the darkness and over to the bungalow in search of her. She was exhausted and cranky. All the good her day off yesterday had done for her was negated by the way she and Casey had ended the night.

Iris peeked out from behind her kitchen curtain and made sure Casey's truck was no longer in sight before she left the house. To be fair, Casey had tried to explain herself during the drive home. But what could she have said to soften the blow from her earlier words? Iris wasn't her type, but she'd do in a pinch.

She felt annoyance rising again, and she grabbed a bag of dried figs and went outside. She had to keep busy and work out some of her anger. Especially since she wasn't sure exactly where that anger should be directed. Toward Casey, who had said the wrong thing? Or toward herself because she had wanted Casey last night and might possibly—just possibly—have been too scared to follow through with her desire.

Iris crinkled the plastic bag of figs as she walked until she heard the loud bleats of the Twins. A moment later, two brown-and-white heads with long, floppy ears poked around the corner of the kennels. Once they spotted her, the Twins came across the yard and toward her in a series of enthusiastic hops.

Iris couldn't help but laugh as they ran to her and begged for treats. She fed them each a few figs before cramming the half-empty bag into her pocket. As soon as the food had disappeared, they lost interest and bounced back the way they had come. She trailed behind and went into the toolshed to get a hammer, nails, and some scrap pieces of wood. She'd finish repairing some of the obstacles in the exercise run today. Casey had nearly completed the work in there, mending the fences and clearing out loose branches and debris. Last week, Iris couldn't look anywhere without seeing an imposing project just waiting to be completed. Now, she had to search to find more cleanup or repair work to do.

Casey's work for the lab and for Iris was about at its end. And she'd be going back to the mainland. Where she belonged, and where she'd find someone who was just right for her—not just right *for now*.

Iris opened the gate to the exercise yard and went over to one of the ramps she used for teaching obedience and obstacle work to her dogs. She had tried to change who she was for other women before. She knew it was a trait she needed to watch carefully in herself, for all the reasons she had explained to Casey last night. She had spent too many years attempting to make her parents see her as their perfect child. The only one they needed. They hadn't, and Iris had been left with a desire to please that could be a hindrance sometimes.

Casey hadn't asked her to change, though. Iris thought about their conversation while she flipped the ramp on its side and inspected a crack caused by a falling limb. She'd need to get a tree person out here to trim away any remaining dead branches before the next earthquake or windstorm brought them down. She pulled off a broken chunk of wood that was meant to be a paw hold for the dogs and replaced it with a new piece.

When she tipped the ramp back to its upright position, she perched on the side of it and remembered Casey's words. She seemed to like Iris. She had merely acknowledged how different they were, something Iris had recognized from the start. Under normal circumstances, she and Casey would never have met, let alone connected the way they had last night.

Would they? What if Iris had walked onto the ferry and found Casey there, headed to a normal vacation on the island? She had a feeling they would have ended up in the same position, kissing in the doorway and contemplating a brief, exciting fling.

Iris stood up and turned toward the next broken obstacle. She let out a surprised yelp when she came face-to-face with Leo, and she nearly knocked the cup of tea out of his hands.

"Jeez, Leo, you almost gave me a heart attack. I'm putting a cat bell on you if I can find a big enough collar."

He laughed and handed her the cup of fragrant, steamy tea. She could smell the citrusy sharpness of her favorite Earl Grey. "If you weren't so distracted, you'd have heard me coming. I even called your name."

"Did not," Iris said. Had he? Her mind had been too full of Casey to notice anything else.

"I startled Casey this morning, too. Seems the two of you have a lot on your minds today."

"Thank you for the tea," Iris said, cradling the cup in her chilled hands and ignoring the implied question in Leo's comment. She liked the thought of Casey being distracted by last night, but she figured it was more likely that Leo had surprised her with his normal stealthy ways, not because she was lost in thoughts of Iris.

Iris took a sip of her tea and balanced the cup on top of a waterproof plastic bin that was full of dog toys. She started to separate the weaving poles into two piles, still-usable ones and broken ones that needed to be replaced. Leo wordlessly began to help her.

"She'll be leaving soon," Iris said, keeping her voice studiously casual.

"Figured. She'll be needing to get back to work."

"Yes. Back to the city." Iris put a little pressure on one of the poles, and it snapped in two. She added it to the discard pile. "I'm sure she'll be glad to get back."

"Huh," Leo said. "Maybe."

Iris gathered the poles they could repair and tucked them under one arm. She picked up her tea with her free hand. She pictured Casey bar hopping in downtown Seattle, dating beautiful women, and enjoying the nightlife. She wanted to break the remaining poles over her knee, but she didn't. "What do you mean, maybe?"

"Seemed to me she likes it here," Leo said. "She's a lot like you."

Iris dropped her armload, and the poles rolled over each other and across the grass. She sighed and put down her tea again. "We're nothing alike."

Leo knelt down to help her pick up the poles. "You're both compassionate and disciplined. And you both are interested in the world. Seemed to me you two had fun together."

"We did, I guess," Iris said noncommittally. Leave it to Leo to strip away their different lifestyles and attitudes and focus instead on the values they shared. Were they enough to justify sex without strings attached? At this point, Iris was wavering toward the side of *yes*.

"I'll work on putting these back together," Leo said, taking the poles and giving her a gentle push toward the dog runs. "You can clean kennels and play with the dogs for a while. It'll clear your head."

Iris started with the two Chihuahuas she had been transporting when she first met Casey. They were exuberant as always when she carefully slipped into their kennel. One of the emails she had answered this morning had been from the Lopez shelter, letting her know the owner had been located and she would be coming to get her dogs later in the afternoon. Iris cleaned their run as well as she could, given all the help they offered.

She watched them tumble and wrestle together like rambunctious siblings. She had told Casey about her parents wanting more children last night, but she hadn't mentioned how much she would have loved to have a sister or brother—or even a whole houseful of them. Not because she had wanted the company or had particularly envied the relationships she saw between her cousins, but because she would have had more freedom. She sometimes felt as if she had spent her childhood under the intense focus of a high-powered microscope. Her parents had clung to her because she was the only one, but at the same time she had felt the resentment and regret that was aimed at her position of only child.

Iris refilled the water bowl the Chihuahuas had knocked over and moved to the next kennel. A much more sedate black Lab waited near the door while she cleaned the floor of the kennel and fluffed his dog bed. He had been at the shelter for over six months after being neglected and then abandoned by his former owner, but just before the earthquake, a family had come to see him after finding his picture online. The oldest child, a boy in his teens, had been aloof during the visit, but the parents and younger child had fallen in love with Blackjack. She hoped they'd call again, and that the dog would find a home with them. She had a feeling the gentle animal would even be able to win over the teenager, who Iris suspected was still grieving the family pet they had lost months ago.

She sat next to the dog when she was done, playing with his soft ears and enjoying his quiet presence. Leo was right, the animals grounded her when she was upset. She had no use for living in the past, and she usually avoided thinking about her childhood unless it was necessary to do so. She had answered Casey's questions about her family because Casey had done the same for her. It was hardly fair to expect her to open up while Iris remained obstinately silent.

And maybe she had wanted Casey to know her better, too.

How much did she want her to know, though? Iris's main form of rebellion had been going to Tacoma's PLU instead of the religious Seattle University her parents preferred. She had lost both of them while she was in her junior year of college—although they had never seemed close in life, they had died within months of each other. She hadn't had a chance to resolve her mixed feelings about their attitude toward her—disappointment mixed with possessive love—and she had never managed to find out if they were proud of her and what she was accomplishing at school. Not that they had ever been either proud of or disappointed in her grades or talents. Nothing had seemed to please them more than her very existence as their child, and nothing was more devastating than her solo status.

Iris got up. Enough wallowing in the past. This was exactly why she didn't want to live there, or in the future. Those roads led to a life of disappointment. She focused on the dogs and the kennels instead, and made her way quickly through the remaining chores.

As soon as she was done, she went back to her house and looked through the shelves in her pantry and fridge. She made a grocery list, planning to fill the empty spaces in her freezer where she had removed meals to share with Casey. She'd shop, cook some food, and finish the illustrations for her spring cards, and be done in time for the evening feeding.

Normalcy. That's exactly what she needed.

❖

Casey had been feeling out of sorts all day. She had briefly contemplated packing her truck and leaving the island before anyone realized she was going, but she hadn't followed through with her plan. Instead, she had gotten up early and had coffee with Leo in the office. Then she had worked in the exercise yard for a few hours before taking Chert out to the woods. Her day followed the rhythm she had discovered here on San Juan Island with one notable exception. Instead of merely checking her seismometers and making any necessary adjustments, she had collected all the instruments and stowed them in the locked box in the bed of her truck.

Chert had been unfazed by her mood, and he had frolicked in the water while she spent almost an hour trying to skip some damned stones across the calm surface of False Bay. He'd spent a happy morning sniffing around while she hunted for fossils in the Ice Age sediments at Cattle Point. Every so often, she told herself to go back to the bungalow and spend the five minutes it would take to pack her clothes and leave, but she made an excuse every time. She still had more rocks to see on San Juan Island, and there were smaller isles to the north and east she'd like to visit if she could charter a boat to take her there. The quiet pace of the islands made them the perfect place to write her paper about her findings.

Casey sighed and found a nook in the rocks where she could eat her lunch shielded from the cool breeze. She shared the ham-and-cheese sandwich she had bought from a convenience store with the dog as she faced the real reason she wasn't prepared to go back to Seattle.

Iris. Casey sensed something unfinished, something hopeful between them. And Chert. Casey rubbed his head and felt some dampness in his fur from his swim. She'd tried to dry him off with a towel, but his coat was too thick for the rectangle of terry cloth. He'd likely spend the afternoon in the bungalow, stretched out close to the warmth of the fire, until he was completely dry and toasty. Casey had gotten used to the odor of heating wet dog in her house, blending with the more pleasant smells from Iris's food.

But it wasn't *her* house. And Chert wasn't her dog. And Iris...well, Iris wasn't her person.

The bungalow, the dog, and Iris would all go on with their lives here once Casey had left. Her space would be taken up by new interns, and Chert would eventually leave with his owners. The signs of the earthquake were already dwindling at the shelter, carted off and stacked on a pile to be burned. She didn't belong here, not like Iris did.

Casey had been wandering this morning, not really doing anything worthwhile besides collecting her instruments. She got up with a sigh and stretched her lower back. Without incoming measurements or fences to repair, she had no excuse for staying. She started walking toward her truck with Chert close behind.

She drove the long way back to Iris's, traveling around the entire island and stopping now and again to walk across crunchy, dried winter grass and stand at the edge of the water. The views changed dramatically as she drove, from Washington's mainland to the smaller islands in the San Juan archipelago, to Canada.

When she finally returned to the shelter, the afternoon was fading to dusk. She parked, and Chert ran ahead of her to the bungalow. He ran down the hall, while she went to the fireplace and started building a fire. She'd stay another night in this cozy little home with the dog for company. Maybe she'd go talk to Iris, try to get them to a more comfortable place before she left. They could write to each other. Skype. Visit.

Or not.

Casey was about to light the kindling when she noticed Chert standing in the hallway and staring at her. Something about the way he was acting made her nervous all of a sudden, and she got up quickly, dropping the box of matches and scattering them across the floor. She hurried down the hall and stepped over the baby gate, looking for the cat under the bed and in the towel-lined box in the closet, but she wasn't there.

Casey clambered back over the gate and went into her bedroom, where she found Chert staring in her closet. She heard a forlorn, low yowl and peered around the closet door, seeing only the shape of the cat on the floor and blood before she stepped back again. She grabbed Chert and coaxed him into the bathroom, shutting the door tightly to keep him from going back into her room. She ran outside and over to Iris's house where she banged on the door until she heard Iris call for her to come in.

"Iris? It's the cat. Something's wrong," she said, gasping, winded from her panicked run even though she hadn't gone more than a few yards. Iris was standing next to her kitchen counter, holding a bag of flour in one hand, but she recovered from her surprise quickly and dropped the flour next to a pile of groceries.

"Come on," she said, jogging out the door. "What happened to her?"

"I don't know," Casey said, willing herself not to cry. "I just got home and found her in my closet. I should have come back earlier. I should have checked on her as soon as I got inside."

"Don't panic," Iris said, climbing the stairs and entering the bungalow. "And don't blame yourself. I checked on her an hour ago and she was under her bed looking normal."

"She's in there," Casey said, pulling Iris's arm to stop her from going to the back bedroom and pointing toward her own room. "In the closet."

Casey stood back while Iris quietly approached the closet and looked inside. She was still for a moment, and then she crouched down just outside the door.

"Is she okay?" Casey asked. She could hear Chert whining from inside the bathroom. "What should I do?"

"Well, for starters, you might want to go online and buy a new sweatshirt," Iris said in a low, non-urgent voice.

"What?"

"A sweatshirt. I doubt you'll want to wear this one anymore. It's covered in kittens."

Iris was grinning at her, so Casey assumed the kittens were alive and well. She went over to the bed and sat down with a thump as the adrenaline coursed through her system with nothing useful to do. She tucked her trembling hands under her thighs. She had been so afraid something was terribly wrong, and she felt something lingering under her relief. Something strangely resembling anger. Why did people get pets when there was always a threat of losing them?

"I saw blood," she said, trying unsuccessfully to keep her voice steady. "I thought she was…"

"She's fine, Casey," Iris said. "Birth can be a messy process, but from what I can see right now, everything seems normal." She paused, with a thoughtful look. "I didn't expect you to be the squeamish type."

"I'm not. At least I don't think I am. I've never really had a chance to find out."

"You've never seen blood before?"

"Of course I have. Just not like this." Casey still felt afraid, an unfamiliar experience for her. And guilty. She should have been here to help with the birth somehow, but given her reaction to a little blood, she figured the cat had been better off without her.

She heard Chert's insistent whine again, but she wasn't sure if she should let him out. Iris got up and unhooked the baby gate, putting it in front of Casey's door instead. She let Chert out of the bathroom, and he stood at the gate with his nose pressed between the bars and his tail waving rhythmically. Casey wanted to look away from him, to keep herself from liking his company and looking forward to taking him in the truck with her, but she couldn't make herself follow logic this time. She got up and knelt by the gate, petting the dog and reassuring him—and herself—that everything was okay.

"I'll be right back," Iris said from the hallway side of the gate. She turned to leave, but Casey called her back.

"Wait, you can't go."

"You'll be fine," Iris said. "I'm only going to the office to get a scale and some forms. You can look at them, you know."

Casey hesitated for a moment, but she was curious because she didn't think she had ever seen a newborn anything. She'd had a couple of friends who had babies, but she hadn't been around them until they were a few months old. She crawled the few steps to the closet door and looked inside. The gray cat regarded her with half-closed eyes, but she didn't seem upset or nervous with Casey there.

Six miniature kittens were stacked in a row, nursing from their mother and making kneading motions with their tiny paws. Casey didn't realize how long she had been staring at them, barely breathing, until she heard Iris's voice.

"Aren't they sweet? I just need to weigh them and check genders, then we'll leave them alone."

She sat cross-legged next to Casey and put the cardboard box from the other bedroom and a small scale with a bowl on top of it between them before reaching into the closet and extracting one of the kittens.

"Is that a kitchen scale?" Casey asked as Iris gently laid the kitten in the bowl and noted its weight on her form.

"Yes. But don't worry, I'll wash it out before I use it to cook food."

"Very comforting. I'll remember that the next time I eat something you've made. Are you taking them away from her?"

Her voice rose slightly as Iris put the little black kitten into the box, and Iris reached over and patted Casey on the knee. "No, I'm not. I'll put the kittens in here, and Momma will follow."

"You sound like you're placating a child," Casey said, swatting playfully at Iris's hand.

"Well, you sound a little like a child." Iris smiled and weighed another kitten. "Do you want to hold one? Just for a few seconds, since they shouldn't be handled much until they're older. And no, you won't hurt her."

Before Casey could protest or run out of the room, Iris nestled the tiny calico in her hands. Casey barely registered her weight, she was so small, but she felt warm, pulsing life transferring through her palms and deep inside her. The kitten was as soft as a handful of cotton balls, and she mewed and stretched with her eyes squinted shut.

Casey looked up and saw Iris watching her, sharing the wonder Casey was feeling. She carefully placed the kitten in the box next to her sister, and the two of them searched blindly for their mother.

"I've never held anything so tiny and alive," Casey said as Iris finished weighing the kittens.

"They're very vulnerable right now," Iris said. She scooted the box into the closet and lifted the gray cat inside where she began licking Casey and Iris cooties off her babies. "They can't see or hear or move very far. They're completely reliant on her and on us. It's a huge responsibility."

Casey nodded as she considered Iris's words. Like most of the things Iris said and wrote, the short sentence seemed to have several possible meanings. Maybe she was talking about her responsibility to the shelter and its residents and what it meant to her. Or maybe she was thinking about human children and parents, continuing the conversations she and Casey had shared the day before.

Casey got to her feet and reached for Iris's hand, pulling her up until they stood close together, facing each other.

"I'm sorry about last night," Casey said. She placed her palm on Iris's neck, feeling both of their heartbeats at once. "I didn't mean to be insulting."

"I know," Iris said. Her voice was barely above a whisper, but Casey felt it vibrate through her palm. "I overreacted. I guess I'm a slow simmer kind of woman, not a bright but short-lived flare. I'm not brave enough for the kind of relationship you offered."

"Not brave? Are you kidding?" Casey laughed and gestured toward the closet with her hand, keeping the other one resting against Iris's skin. She felt power and passion just under the surface, but Iris didn't seem ready to set them free. "You had no idea what you'd find in that closet, especially after I freaked out in your kitchen, but you didn't hesitate to go in there. You were ready to do whatever had to be done. You're very brave, Iris."

Casey wanted to kiss her, to repeat last night with a different ending this time, but she wasn't ready to be rejected again. And she couldn't promise anything more than a few days or hours together.

She kissed Iris's forehead instead, and then stepped away, dragging her hand away from Iris as if it had a will of its own and would rather stay close to her.

"Brave is knowing what you want and not accepting anything less," Casey said.

CHAPTER FIFTEEN

What *did* she want? Iris asked herself the question over and over during the night, but she wasn't comfortable with her answers. She was the one who had pushed Casey away, and she was the one who could bridge the gap between them if she chose to. She had felt it in Casey's touch last night, as the weight of her hand had rested against Iris's neck, pouring strength and desire into Iris's bloodstream like a transfusion.

So why was she hesitating? She wanted Casey. She didn't necessarily want a permanent relationship—she was busy enough as it was with her shelter and her cards. She didn't honestly believe Casey was treating her like a convenient warm body, but instead she felt that Casey was as surprised by their mutual attraction as she was. Casey just had the guts to make a move. Iris wasn't sure she could do the same.

Casey was probably long gone, anyway, she told herself as she left the house and headed toward the bungalow to check on the kittens. Casey wasn't in the small house, but there were signs of her continued presence at the shelter—a sweater draped across a kitchen stool and a pile of gray stones on the counter. Iris laughed to herself. Surely Casey wouldn't leave such treasures behind.

Iris peeked at the cat. She was curled in a ball and sound asleep with her six kittens tucked on all sides. Her food and water bowls were full and close to the box. Iris backed out of the room quietly and went back through the kitchen. She paused by the counter for a moment and picked up one of the rocks. It looked like nothing special, nothing she didn't see thousands of times a day in her garden or on the beach, but she was sure Casey had a story for each rock in the pile.

Iris picked them up one by one and imagined Casey's voice spinning stories for them. This one had probably lined the first campfire ever created by a Neanderthal, and this one might have come from the first crack during the big bang. Iris smiled. Casey was a scientist and knew the real history of these stones, but she was a storyteller, too. She saw beauty and romance in the past.

Iris pictured Casey as she had looked last night, with awe and wonder in her expression as she held the tiny calico in her hands. Casey studied the past, the history of the earth written in the shape of the islands and the minerals contained in them, but how much time did she spend in the present, with living beings? She made friends easily and seemed to have connected with the locals, but she had a distance about her when she was with other people. It disappeared when she was in the field, talking about her beloved quartz and feldspar. Iris had seen hints of the same engagement when Casey was with Chert and when she had watched the gray cat and her kittens.

And when she had kissed Iris. Casey had been right there with her, borderless and open. Iris needed to realize what a gift that was. Casey wasn't offering forever, but she was offering something she seemed to hold close most of the time.

Maybe Iris would take a chance and continue the conversation she and Casey had begun in Friday Harbor. She claimed to live in the present—why not make it a wonderful one, even if only for a few hours?

Maybe. If Casey was still around after Iris finished her work. Or maybe tonight, if Casey was still here after dinner.

Or maybe tomorrow, if Casey hadn't left the island.

Iris sighed as she walked up the path to the converted barn where all the cats lived. She risked continuing with her maybes until Casey was a distant memory.

Iris went through the first door and into the tiny foyer, barely big enough for two people but large enough to do the job of preventing a cat escape. She closed the door firmly behind her and went through the second door. A chorus of meows greeted her, and she nearly tripped as four cats wound around her ankles.

She hurried to get bowls of food on the ground before any squabbles broke out among the feline residents, and then she slowed down and did a more thorough check of the rooms and the cats. The barn had been on the property when Iris bought it, but it had been badly in need of repair and only used for storage. Now it was insulated and heated, with running water, a small kitchen, and a room where they could treat sick or injured animals and keep them safely isolated from the others. She had a few antisocial cats who were kept in a separate area in the back of the barn, but most of the shelter cats lived in the large main space that was full of climbing toys and soft places to sleep. Cat House duty wasn't the most pleasant, with what seemed like miles of litter boxes to clean twice a day, but Iris had never heard anyone complain about the job. She had to make a rotating schedule when there were interns on the property—not because she had to force them to work in here, but because she wanted to give everyone a fair chance to have time with the cats.

Iris systematically worked her way through the chore list, cleaning food bowls, freshening water, and scooping boxes. She tried to keep on task, but the cats distracted her as they always did. Balls of fluff went tumbling and wrestling by her feet every time she walked from one end of the room to the other, and some of the more playful cats swiped at her hands every time they moved. Iris felt the stretch of a smile on her face whenever she was in here.

When she finished the to-do list, she lingered for a few minutes and visited with the cats. She was meticulous about keeping the room clean because of the number of them in here. The room never reeked of unchanged litter, but the air was always heavy with the smell of animal and fur. She was lucky she didn't suffer from allergies. Otherwise, she'd need an epinephrine shot every time she walked into the barn.

Iris picked up an orange cat and held it close, feeling its purrs rumbling through her. She was getting more calls every day from people who were returning to the islands and searching for lost pets. After talking to more than one owner who had been frantic about their animals but unable to locate them in the shelter system, Iris had come up with a plan for creating a single database she and the humane society and the other shelters could use to spread the word about the animals they had rescued. If there was another disaster or earthquake— or, as Casey would insist, *when* there was another one—Iris and others like her would be prepared to communicate with each other and with owners.

But people were slowly finding her. And most likely, Chert's owners would eventually be among them. Casey had been adamant about not being able to have a dog in the city, whether as a preemptive strike against getting attached to Chert or because her lifestyle really wouldn't let her have him, but maybe she could have a cat. Something warm and soft waiting for her at home, but an easier pet for a busy apartment dweller to handle than a large and active dog.

Iris gave the orange cat one more hug, and then she let him loose among his friends. Maybe she'd bring up the cat idea, if Casey was still around later today. The little calico would be looking for a good home once she was old enough to leave her mother...

With all her big plans about what she'd do if Casey stuck around, Iris wasn't sure if she should feel pleased or anxious when she got back to the kennel and saw Casey in the exercise yard with Chert. She stood by the gate for a few minutes and watched Casey trying to lure the dog up the ramp with a treat. He went around and under the ramp without hesitation, even hopping over the low end once, but he refused to step on it. He seemed happy, lolling his tongue out to one side and dropping into play posture whenever Casey tapped her hand on the ramp. Casey looked a little frustrated.

"He thinks it's a game," Iris said, opening the gate and walking into the yard. "He doesn't realize you want him to do something in particular."

Casey smiled when she turned and saw Iris approaching. "I'd climb up there myself and show him, but we just repaired these obstacles. I don't want to do it again."

"Just make your intention more obvious. Here, let me have some of those treats." Iris took a few of the small bone-shaped training treats from Casey and walked several yards away from the ramp. "Chert, come," she said, making the words bright and clear. She gave him one treat when he trotted to her and let him sniff the others in her hand.

"Come," she repeated, running toward the ramp with her hand out to her side. She jogged close to the obstacle with her treat-filled hand marking the path she wanted the dog to take, and he followed the treats up and over the narrow ramp. She made a fuss of him on the other side and gave him the treats. "Good boy!"

"Show-off," Casey said. She pushed Iris playfully aside. "Let me try."

"Don't hesitate when you get there," Iris called encouragingly. "You don't want to give him a chance to veer off course."

Casey rolled her eyes at the instructions, but she did exactly what Iris said, and Chert trotted easily over the obstacle.

Iris walked slowly over to where the two were celebrating Chert's great achievement. She barely remembered what Casey had been like when she first got to the shelter. Hesitant around the animals and uncertain about what to do with the dog she had rescued. Now she was comfortable and relaxed with him and all the others at the shelter. Iris wondered if Casey still recognized herself.

"I'm going to Vancouver Island for a couple hours today," Iris said. She knelt next to the pair. "A friend of mine is flying there to visit his daughter and said he'd take me to do a home check for a family that wants to adopt the black Lab. If you want to come, I'd like to take you out to lunch after."

She intentionally phrased it like she was asking Casey on a date, not because she wanted to send her a message about her intention, but because she didn't want to give herself a chance to back out and turn the afternoon into something else. Something less.

"You'd need your passport," she added when the silence stretched between them.

"I'll go get it." Casey rested her hand on Chert's neck. "And see if Leo will take care of this guy."

Her voice was casual, not betraying any emotion about Iris's offer or questioning what she meant by it, but as Casey walked by her on the way out of the exercise yard, she brushed her shoulder against Iris's. On its own, the contact was nothing much. Clothes between them, no exchange of intimate words or knowing glances. But Iris felt a jolt of awareness in Casey's touch. All her hesitation melted away. Now that she had initiated the journey, the next steps didn't seem so difficult to take.

Iris drove them to the Friday Harbor airport. She had expected to feel awkward with the shift she felt in their relationship, but they chatted easily as Iris pointed out some of her favorite places on the island.

"What made you come here?" Casey asked. "Was this a favorite vacation spot or something?"

Iris laughed. "Actually, I'd never been here before I came and bought the shelter. I grew up in Auburn, near Seattle, and then went to school in Tacoma. I even stayed at the same college for graduate work." Iris paused. Her life sounded boring to her. Her family hadn't traveled beyond the state lines, and she'd been busy with school, work, and then the shelter since leaving home. "I guess that sounds dull to you."

"Why? I'm not exactly a jet-setter. I travel a little for my work, and I moved from Chicago to California, then to Washington, but I don't tend to go far. I go deep. I think you do, too, although you go deeper into the community and I go into the earth and the past."

Iris reached across Casey's lap, admittedly lingering along the way, and got a notebook from the glove compartment. "Write that down," she said, tossing it on Casey's lap.

"Did I inspire a poem or a greeting card?" Casey asked with a laugh, but she pulled the pen out of the spiral edge of the notebook and wrote quickly.

"I'm not sure yet. I don't have much demand for geology cards." She held up her hand, palm facing Casey. "And please don't start on the rock puns again."

Casey closed the notebook. "You still haven't answered my question about how you decided to come here."

Iris shrugged and turned off the road and into the airport's parking lot. "I worked in a shelter during college. I hadn't been around animals much either, but my roommate wanted to be a vet and she volunteered with a rescue center. I ended up getting more involved than I expected, and I started to connect with other shelter workers online. A friend I'd met on a rescue website mentioned she was selling this place and retiring. By then, I was almost finished with college and I could get the graduate degree I wanted through a distance program. I'd already started making decent money for my cards, so I was thinking of buying a house."

Iris parked her car and let the engine idle while she thought back to her last year in college. She had spent her life feeling slightly resentful of the all-encompassing disappointment of her parents and the resulting realization that she wouldn't make them proud unless she developed the technology needed to clone herself. "I always felt stifled by my parents' rules and expectations, but I guess those rules gave me an excuse for not taking monumental chances in life. Even after they died, I took the easiest path available and planned to stay at the same school for my master's degree. I didn't really have any other place to call home."

Iris hated admitting all this to Casey, but she finished the story. "I'd only seen pictures of the San Juans and the property, but it looked like a nice place to live. I suppose I could have moved anywhere in the world, but I just took the opportunity that presented itself. I made an offer, and she accepted, and now I'm here."

Iris felt Casey's fingers on her chin, making Iris turn and look at her. She was smiling and shaking her head.

"For someone with such a talent for using words, you suck at telling stories about yourself."

Iris started to protest, but Casey spoke before she could.

"You support yourself and all these animals with a creative and interesting career. You took a chance and moved here without knowing what to expect, which takes guts and a lot of faith. You've made a difference in your community and in the lives of every dog and cat and goat you've rescued and re-homed. And like it or not, you're a gifted poet. Don't ever sell yourself short, Iris."

Iris put her hand over Casey's where it still rested on her chin and gave her fingers a squeeze. She loved her life, but she always assumed it looked boring from the outside, especially to someone like Casey. She didn't *need* the validation, but she appreciated it.

They sat quietly in the warmth of the car with their fingers entwined softly. Everything about their kiss two nights ago had been electric, but today—asking Casey out, their conversation, and now these moments of unspoken companionship—their movements together were slow and gentle, as if they were taking a deep breath together before tonight. Iris had no doubt their passion would flash like lightning when they were ready for it, but she loved the calm of these shared moments before the storm.

She eventually noticed the time. "Sean will be waiting for us," she said, reluctantly lowering her hand and opening the car door. "We should go."

Casey got out of the car and walked beside her toward the cluster of hangars. Iris led them between two of the low, wide buildings and onto the tarmac border along the runway. She waved at Sean, who was fiddling with something on the wing of his little Piper. Iris walked several steps before she realized Casey was no longer next to her. She retraced her steps.

"What's wrong?"

"That's a small plane."

"Yes," Iris said slowly. "Smaller than a jumbo jet. But big enough for the three of us. Don't tell me you're afraid to fly."

Casey made a scoffing sound that would have been more convincing if she had seemed willing to move forward and toward the plane.

"I'm not afraid. I just don't like to fly. There's a difference."

"Of course there is," Iris said soothingly. She took Casey's arm and pulled her forward. "Let's go."

Sean was waiting for them. Iris had flown with him plenty of times, so he turned his attention to Casey and gave her a complete tour of the plane. Casey smiled and asked a few questions, but she looked a little green. Iris remembered her saying she had been on a plane when the earthquake hit, and she nudged Casey aside as Sean was climbing in the cockpit.

"We can stay here, if you'd rather," she said. "I can do the home check another time."

Casey shook her head. "No, I'm all right. Let's get this over with."

CHAPTER SIXTEEN

F ront or back?"
"Back, I guess," Casey said. It might buy her a few precious seconds if the tiny plane nosedived into the ground. She had never been fond of flying, starting with her first time on an airplane mere hours after her mother's funeral, but if she had to do it, she preferred a little more size and substance.

"Are you sure?" Iris caught her arm as she was about to climb through the hobbit-sized door of the plane. "If you sit up front, Sean might let you take the controls for a while. It's a blast."

"The back. Definitely the back," Casey said disengaging herself from Iris's hold and getting in the plane. Sean was a big guy and his bulk took up most of the cockpit. Iris looked very slight next to him, so hopefully they wouldn't be over the weight limit. Given the size of the Piper, Casey figured the limit was about fifty pounds. She scrunched close to the window and tried to think light and airy thoughts.

Sean taxied to the end of the runway and idled there while he went through an elaborate series of preflight checks. Iris pointed to various instruments and seemed to be asking questions about them, but Casey couldn't hear their words over the noise of the engine until Sean reached back and handed her a headphone set.

Once she had it on, she could hear them, but she had to lean forward at an odd angle for the cord to be plugged in. Iris's and Sean's voices sounded tinny and remote, and the number of instruments they discussed only made her realize how much could potentially go wrong while they were in the air.

She took the headphones off and leaned back instead, staring over the plane's wing at the border of trees that marked the edge of the runway. She spent most of her life performing the role of a scientist and trying to figure out how things worked, but in some instances, she didn't really want to know the details. Like flying. She preferred her pilots to handle flaps and fuel mixtures behind the closed door of a cockpit while she handled a gin and tonic and her tray table.

As soon as Sean aimed the little plane down the long stretch of the runway and tossed them into the air with a jolt, Casey was happily distracted by the airborne view she had of San Juan and the northern islands. Since they stayed low on the short hop to Vancouver Island, Casey had a chance to see the details of some formations. She pressed closer to the window, not minding the flight as much as she had before. She was about to tap Iris on the shoulder and point out the dipping sandstone beds on Spieden Island when she realized Iris seemed to actually be flying the plane.

Casey wasn't sure how she felt about this. She'd trust Iris with a lot of things. Dog training, dinner prep, kitten delivery. But flying? She hadn't mentioned having a pilot's license or any sort of training. In fact, when she had mentioned Sean letting Casey fly if she was up front, she had implied that he'd hand the controls over to anyone sitting in the seat next to him without checking credentials or putting the person through hours of ground school before the flight. Casey pried her fingers off the seat. She had to admit, Iris was doing fine. The plane was level, not plummeting toward the Nanaimo sandstone outcropping below them on Waldron Island. The engines weren't sputtering, and nothing was on fire.

She admittedly wasn't the most enthusiastic airplane passenger, but she usually didn't feel this jumpy and out of control. She watched Iris's profile with her delicate features and gentle tilt of a smile on her face. She scanned the horizon constantly, with an intense concentration, but she seemed at ease at the same time.

Casey had been calm on the outside but jumping up and down thrilled on the inside when Iris asked her to come today. She understood the message behind the request for a date. Casey had made an offer for a short-term, fun form of intimacy and Iris—even though she had rejected it at first—had made the decision to accept. No pretending, no lying, and no commitment beyond the next day or two. Or three…

Maybe three days, and then she would get on the ferry and leave the island, Chert, and Iris behind. Casey wouldn't lie to Iris, and she couldn't lie to herself. She was going to miss all three. She figured this was why she was nervous about Iris's willingness to explore their attraction. She wanted her of course, but she would be adding a few more strings to the already tangled knots holding her in this place. She knew she would be sad when she left, but she didn't have any real experience leaving someone or something behind—except for the transition to Chicago after her mother died. Casey couldn't predict how hard it would be for her to leave, and that scared the hell out of her. The unknown needed to be studied, cataloged, and explained. In this case, she couldn't anticipate what her own reaction would be.

But she would survive the pain of leaving. She'd return to her job, to the paper she was writing, and to the distracting clamor of the city, and she'd manage to get past whatever uncomfortable emotions she might feel at first. She'd get through it because, for damned sure, she wasn't going to reject anything Iris might offer.

Casey looked back over her shoulder and saw a hazy silhouette of the city of Vancouver, on Canada's mainland north and slightly behind them. She put her faith in Iris and enjoyed the scenery spread out below and around her. She saw tree-lined, rocky islands, but she also noticed the evidence of glacial erosion and seismic activity in the shape and position of the landforms. She took her mind off the plane and thoughts of Iris naked and instead pictured the ancient forces that had gouged out the Sound. She looked out the window at the present, but she really was seeing huge sheets of ice scraping away at the islands and hearing the rumble as parts of the earth's crust slid against each other, creating the folds and faults she knew were hidden by the thick blanket of conifers.

Pretty soon, the scene shifted from one of blue-gray water dotted with tree-covered natural islands to the larger mass of Vancouver Island. As the ground below them became more populated, the skies did as well. Casey noticed a small seaplane skimming just below them and she put the headset back on just as Sean was taking control of the plane again. Iris turned around and grinned at Casey. Her obvious pleasure in the trip and having Casey with her almost made Casey forget her concern about being in a collision. Almost.

She hadn't expected to see actual full-sized planes, but jets and propeller planes of all shapes and sizes were either circling the airport or filtering into a line and landing. Casey heard the static-y voice of someone in the control tower give Sean some unintelligible instructions and a list of numbers. Casey wasn't sure what it meant until he spoke to her and Iris.

"We're cleared to land right away if we can squeeze between these two 737s," he said. "Just a quick drop here. Be a mite bumpy."

Casey felt the little plane dip and turn at the same time, half a second after her mind processed Sean's warning. She'd have been more than happy to circle the airport a few minutes or hours longer if it had meant avoiding the stomach-dropping maneuver, but Sean neatly slotted them into the gap between the two large jets. His landing was smooth, but Casey was flung against the restraint of her seat belt yet again when he veered sharply off the runway, presumably to avoid being squished by the plane following them. Her shoulder and hipbones smarted from the tight grip of the nylon belt, but they were on the ground and alive.

Iris got out of the plane and held out her hand to help Casey. She wedged herself through the door and held Iris's hand lightly as she jumped to the tarmac.

"Great flight, wasn't it?" Iris gave her a quick kiss on the cheek, clearly still thrilled about handling the controls. Casey was struggling to keep herself from lying prone on the tarmac and kissing the ground in gratitude.

"Yeah. Especially that last part, where Sean was auditioning for a spot with the Blue Angels."

He laughed. "The feeling that you're out of control can make you nervous. We'll have you sit up front on the way back and do a little flying. You'll feel more relaxed if you take charge for a few minutes."

"Actually, I was thinking of swimming back to the island. It doesn't look that far, and I haven't been exercising much lately…"

Iris and Sean laughed like she was making a joke. "You'll love it, Casey. Flying is very empowering."

Casey just smiled and nodded. She'd let them think she was going along with this insane plan. She was sure there'd be plenty of opportunities for her to escape and take the frigid water route instead.

Iris kept hold of her hand as they left Sean with the plane and walked over to the terminal, either to stay close or because she sensed Casey was planning to make a break for the open waters. They got through customs before the passengers on the jets had deplaned, and then went back outside to the car Iris had rented.

Casey didn't want the contact between her and Iris to stop, and she kept the flat of her palm resting on Iris's thigh while she read the directions and Iris drove to the potential adopter's house. Maybe it was the near-death experience of the small plane ride driving her, but she had a sudden and acute awareness of time ticking between them. She knew it was going to be harder to leave once she let more barriers down, but she had an even stronger desire to make the most of what they had.

"We won't be here long," Iris said when they pulled up in front of a blue house with white trim. "I just want to see the yard and house and make sure Blackjack is going to a good home. Then we can get lunch in town."

"With plenty of alcohol to help me through the return flight," Casey finished for her. She slowly pulled her hand away from Iris's thigh, putting some pressure on her fingertips as they grazed against the rough denim.

"Or we can skip lunch and see how fast Sean can get us back to the island." Iris's voice deepened slightly and Casey smiled in response.

"I've heard that chartered boats are even faster than planes," Casey offered as they got out of the car and walked up the path leading to the house. "Faster and safer."

Iris laughed and rang the doorbell. A small boy answered the door before Casey could protest that she really wasn't joking about searching for an alternative form of transportation.

"Did you bring our dog?" the boy asked, scanning the empty space behind Iris and Casey.

"Not yet," Iris said. "He asked me to come here first, to make sure you're ready to have him come home."

Casey felt a strange sense of disconnect as soon as they walked into the house. She couldn't help but wonder if Iris would do a home check like this for Chert one day, if his owners never claimed him. The new people would probably change his name. And they might not figure out the exact spot behind his right ear where he loved to be scratched.

Casey sat on the edge of the couch and listened as the parents tearfully told the story of losing their family pet a year ago and finally feeling ready to welcome another one into their house. The home was perfect, with a bed and dog bowls and toys already in place and ready for the Lab. The yard was fenced and grassy, complete with a spirited little boy for Blackjack to play with. The entire situation was about as far as one could get from Casey's cramped city apartment.

She distracted herself from the threatening gloom of sadness by watching the couple's older son Chris during the interview. He seemed awkward and nervous as he tried to maintain the bored façade required of a teenager. While they were inspecting the yard and Iris was distracted by the younger boy's incessant questions, Casey quietly moved over to where the teen was leaning against the sliding glass door with an ineffective air of indifference.

"Queenie was your dog, wasn't she?" Casey asked. The parents and the little boy, Kyle, had been weepy during the story of her illness, but Chris had remained nearly expressionless. Casey had at first thought he seemed cold, but then she saw signs indicating what a tremendous effort he was making to seem that way, with his tight jaw, reddening eyes that wouldn't remain focused on any one object for more than a few seconds, and hands clenched tightly in his lap.

He nodded but didn't look at her. "My parents got her when I was a baby," he said simply, and Casey filled in the rest of the story, the years of play and companionship they had shared. She guessed that he was feeling some resentment right now, because his younger brother was just starting a journey that had ended for him last year. She also suspected that he had missed having a dog and a part of him was excited to have another one in the house. Of course, if those suspicions were correct, then he must have a large dose of guilt added to the mix. She wondered if there was a way to help him get to a point where he could accept the new animal into his life.

"She sounds like she was a wonderful dog. Look, I know you can never replace her, and that you don't even want to try. But she had a great home here where she was loved and happy. Blackjack's never had a place like this or a family like yours."

While she had worked at the shelter with Leo, he had shared stories about the animals she met and had shown her pictures of how they looked when they were first brought to Iris's place. She knew what it would mean for the dog to be here. She especially knew what it would mean to Iris to place one of her beloved animals in a forever home.

"You can love him, you know, and no one would ever think you've forgotten Queenie. They'll just think how great it is for Blackjack to finally be somewhere safe, with a new family."

He cleared his throat like he was about to speak, but he just gave her a jerky nod instead and walked back into the house. Iris and the parents looked up with worried faces when he left, and all Casey could do was shrug. She didn't know if she'd said the right things or the completely wrong ones.

She didn't see him again before they left, but Iris and the rest of the family made plans for her to bring Blackjack the next weekend. Casey would be back on the mainland by then, but she wished she could see the look on Kyle's face when his dog arrived, and see if Chris was able to welcome the new family pet with a little enthusiasm.

She told Iris about their conversation on their way to Victoria. "I'll bet you would have known exactly what to tell him," Casey said. She was leaning toward Iris, with her arm resting on the back of Iris's seat. If she just stretched her fingers a little, they'd tangle in Iris's hair. She stayed where she was, though, enjoying the anticipatory feeling of being close without actually touching. Sensing some sort of current sparking between them even though there wasn't any point of contact.

Iris shook her head and a few strands of hair brushed Casey's hand. "I doubt it. You gave him an opportunity to see Blackjack's arrival from the dog's point of view, not through the haze of his own pain and guilt. It's almost like you gave him permission to like Blackjack when his grief might have kept him from being able to do so, because he deserves to have a nice home."

"Maybe you can let me know what happens when you deliver him." This was the first time Casey had made any mention of future contact between her and Iris. She stayed perfectly still, wondering how Iris would react and trying to figure out how she felt about the comment. Did she want to keep in touch? Or would it only hurt worse if they let the relationship linger?

"I'll let you know how it goes," Iris said after a brief pause. She remained quiet then, navigating through the increasingly heavy traffic as they reached downtown Victoria.

The town had a quaint, European feel to it, with delicate wrought-iron lampposts and ivy-covered buildings, but with bright, contemporary touches as well. Within several blocks, Casey saw a white, clean-lined shopping center at the marina on one side of the street and the elegant Empress Hotel on the other. Horse-drawn carriages ambled down the sidewalk past galleries with modern abstract sculptures and paintings displayed in the windows.

"It's coming back to life," Iris said as she slowed down to pass a carriage covered with flowers like a parade float. "The earthquake did as much damage here as in the San Juans, but you can barely see the effects of it anymore. Except that there aren't as many pedestrians as usual."

She turned onto a side street and parked the car before leading Casey to a small café with a view of the harbor. They held hands again, as naturally as if they'd been dating for weeks. Casey couldn't remember when she'd felt such a sense of comfort, due to the wonderful feel of having Iris close and to the welcoming and accepting feeling she sensed in the town.

Whatever happened, however difficult it would be to say good-bye, this trip had been good for her. She was breathing more deeply here. She had been tightly wrapped in a cocoon for a long time, but she had shed it layer by layer until the claustrophobic feeling she had become accustomed to was gone.

They sat near the window bordered with yellow eyelet fabric curtains and next to a cabinet displaying a collection of blue-and-white Spode china. Prompted by Casey's questions, Iris described her visits to Victoria during the height of tourist season while they waited for their lunch.

"I had afternoon tea at the Empress once. Very luxurious. A friend of mine from college married her girlfriend in the rose garden at the hotel and the reception started with a formal tea. Champagne, teensy cucumber sandwiches, and a bowl of local blueberries covered with cream. Yum. I practically begged our waitress for the scone recipe, but she said the chef wouldn't tell. I smuggled one out in my pocket so I could remember what it was like and recreate it."

Casey laughed at the image of Iris stuffing her pockets with food during a fancy tea party. "What else did you take? A snack for later in the evening?"

"Just some chocolate cake, a handful of cookies, and some crustless chicken salad sandwiches. Dancing makes me hungry."

"Those must have been some deep pockets." Casey reached across the table and wrapped her fingers around Iris's.

"I wore an overcoat just in case," Iris said with a laugh as she rubbed her thumb across Casey's palm. Casey's ability to breath deep seemed to vanish, wiped away by Iris's touch. Iris let go when the food arrived and Casey exhaled with a sigh.

Casey took a sip of her Viennese coffee with its hints of cocoa powder and almond syrup. The scent of the sweet coffee mingled with the heavier brie and chutney from her panini to make an almost perfect combination. She wondered if she should have picked the one Iris had instead, though. Would mozzarella and sun-dried tomatoes blend better with the almond flavor?

"Are you eyeballing my sandwich?" Iris asked. She took a sip of her tea but kept one hand defensively in front of her plate.

"Maybe," Casey admitted. "Don't worry, though. I'm not going to grab it from you. I was just wondering how it would taste with my coffee."

"We can share half and half if you want. I don't want a repeat of the pot roast incident."

Casey laughed. "Only a small piece of potato fell on the floor. And that wouldn't have happened if you hadn't stabbed at me with your fork."

"Remember that the next time you contemplate stealing my food. Here." She handed Casey half of her panini and swapped it for one with brie.

Casey spent the rest of the meal laughing and talking with Iris, but a small part of her mind was preoccupied with the exchange. It was such a *couple* thing to do, like holding hands or sharing inside jokes. Why did it make her nervous to act this way with Iris? She wasn't supposed to want these things, these indications of closeness. They weren't things you could measure or trust, and they weren't going to last because Iris was here and Casey mentally already had one foot back in Seattle, straddling the gulf of space between them.

She took a bite of Iris's sandwich, enjoying the mouthwatering tartness of the sun-dried tomato and how good it tasted in combination with the chutney from the other half.

Sharing like this was easy with lunch. The rest of the time? That's when it got hard.

Chapter Seventeen

Iris sat in the back of the plane on the way home and alternated between writing ideas for greeting cards and watching Casey suffer through a flight lesson from Sean. She didn't look nearly as ecstatic as Iris felt when she got to fly. Iris had seen quite a few different sides of Casey on this short trip. She was a kaleidoscope of colors and moods, bright and changeable and full of movement.

She drew a sketch of a solitary person walking along a beach and quickly wrote a free verse note of condolence to go with it. She usually stayed away from bereavement cards because they seemed depressing to her and she never knew what to write. She had a difficult time looking beyond the sadness of the moment, but hearing how Casey had talked to Chris today inspired her. She could see the seeds of hope and possibility Casey planted, and she wanted to capture the same hint of the future while still respecting the pain experienced by the people receiving the cards.

She managed to finish five sample cards by the time they landed, only two of which had black slashes across them from the times the plane had bounced in turbulence and made her lose control of her pencil. She packed her supplies away and got off the plane. After thanking Sean, she and Casey walked back to her car. She draped her arm across Casey's shoulders, matching her pace and steps to Casey's.

"Did you feel better on this part of the trip?"

"Better, as in even more relieved to be alive?" Casey asked. "If so, then yes."

Iris bumped Casey with her hip and sent her a few steps off course. "I meant better, as in less scared by the wee little plane." She ended the sentence in a high baby-talk tone.

"You'd better watch out," Casey said, looking like she wanted to keep her face stern, but laughing instead. "I'll find something you don't like and see how you feel about getting up close and personal with it. How are you with spiders?"

"Love them."

"Snakes?"

Iris put her bag in the backseat and got in the car. "Nature's mousetraps. I'd have a dozen as pets if I had the space."

Casey thought for a moment. "Heights?"

"Isn't that one of yours? Or would you be just as nervous in a plane that's taxiing along the ground?"

"It's not the height. I've scaled cliffs before, and it's never bothered me."

"What is it about flying, then?" On the list of Casey facets she had seen today, her tension associated with the plane trip had been the most curious to Iris. Casey seemed good at keeping her emotions private, and Iris had a feeling that she could have seemed cool as a seasoned pilot during their trip if she'd chosen to. But she had let Iris see her weakness. Maybe because she wanted them to be closer, and she wasn't trying to hide from Iris. Or maybe she was just confident and strong enough to feel comfortable in those moments when she wasn't.

"I don't really know what it is. Sean might be partly right about the loss of control. My first time in a plane was horrible, and I guess you never forget the feeling."

Iris laced her fingers with Casey's, their hands resting on Casey's lap. "Why was it bad?"

Casey looked out the passenger window and exhaled with a puff of air. "My grandparents had come to get me after my mom died. Dad had a work conference or something so he wasn't there, and I was with these two people I'd never met before. Everything was awful. I had been crying for days and flying hurt my sinuses. I had only met my father a few times, so I was basically leaving home to live with strangers."

Iris glanced over at Casey and saw a frown drawing her eyebrows together. "It's all a fog of pain and sadness," Casey said. "I think I remember asking for a dog on the plane, but I don't know why I would have asked then. I guess I was confused by all the changes."

A small child, with her whole world ripped out from under her. Iris was surprised Casey handled flying as well as she did, given her early experience with it. She lifted their joined hands and brushed her lips across Casey's knuckles.

The gesture was easy to make, given how unfamiliar it was for Iris. She thought back to old girlfriends and couldn't remember touching them like this, offering unspoken support. She had tended to date women who didn't need anything from her because she had spent too many years failing to meet expectations and she was tired of it. But where she'd expected to find mutual independence, she had instead found women who decided *she* was the needy one. They would breeze into her life and try to make her something she wasn't. Iris usually made a weak effort to change—more to keep a sense of peace between them than because she believed she needed to. The transformation never lasted long, though. She was Iris.

She was always going to be Iris.

Casey, however, made her *more* Iris. Just like she saw different sides to Casey, she had been noticing more dimensions of her own coming to light since they had met. They were all recognizable to her, and not someone else's idea of who she should be.

She was writing more poetry these days. Cooking was fun again, not just a fill-the-freezer chore. Iris had also been inspired by their trip to Orcas. She was quite aware she'd never have the same degree of interest in piles of rocks that Casey had, but she had recaptured her love for these islands and the opportunities they offered for finding peace and beauty in nature. She needed to get out on the island more, taking the shelter dogs on hikes and for runs on the beach.

She felt a twist of sadness inside. Casey had helped her rediscover these passions, and Iris was determined not to lose them again, but she'd be on her own from here on. She didn't need Casey to motivate her, of course, but she had more fun with her than she did alone. She liked sharing meals with Casey and fighting over scraps like two hungry dogs, watching her expression change as she read Iris's poetry, and learning interesting bits and pieces about the geologic history of the island.

Casey squeezed her hand as if sensing Iris's lonely thoughts. She might be having them, too. Iris had absolutely no doubt that Casey would miss things about being on the island. She clearly loved Chert and the other residents, and Iris had even caught her sneaking treats to the Twins. She obviously liked Iris's company, and the attraction between them was undeniable. Iris had long suspected that Casey's life in Seattle was likely filled with noise and busyness, but not a lot of warmth and companionship like she'd found at the shelter.

They drove the last few minutes of the short drive in a silence filled with soft touches and constant contact. When they got back to the shelter, Casey got out of the car and gave a shrill whistle. Iris heard an answering woof, and then the clatter of pebbles as Chert tore around the corner of the kennels and across the gravel lot to greet Casey. He skidded over to Iris for some attention before running back to Casey and sitting close by her side.

"Feeding time?" Casey asked.

"Soon." Iris nodded. "I should check the kittens first, though." Both Leo and Agatha had sent her text updates throughout the afternoon, but Iris wanted to see all the animals for herself.

The three of them went into the bungalow, and Chert waited on his side of the baby gate while Iris and Casey looked in on the gray cat and her nursing litter. Casey reached in and ran a gentle finger over the furry bodies, and Iris stood behind her with a hand on her shoulder. Casey straightened and turned, catching Iris around the waist before she could step back. Casey pulled her into a hug, and Iris felt her give a trembling sigh.

"Thank you," Casey whispered close to her ear, so quietly that Iris wasn't sure if she heard the words or merely felt their vibrations.

"For the harrowing plane ride, or for lunch?"

Casey shrugged against her, and Iris wanted to moan with pleasure as the movement made Casey's breasts brush against hers.

"For all of this," Casey said.

"You're welcome." Iris wanted to say more. To ask Casey not to leave. To warn her about how much she was going to miss the shelter that was full of life. But she couldn't. Maybe she was wrong, and once Casey was back in the city she'd have a full life waiting for her. Parties, places to go, women to date. Iris needed to be here, but maybe Casey had just enjoyed it as a change of pace.

Casey pulled out of the hug in achingly slow motion until they were nose to nose, and Iris felt each fraction of a millimeter of skin as Casey's cheek slid along hers. Casey's fingers brushed through her hair, sifting through the strands and letting them fall against her cheekbones. With the same unhurried pace, Casey leaned closer until her lips pressed against Iris's in a kiss that felt more reverent than passionate. The scent of Casey filled Iris's whole being with the sensation of being in the woods after a rain. Fresh and earthy, with spruce and the merest hint of a raindrop falling off a flower petal.

Iris made a surprising sound, almost a growl, and wrapped her arms around Casey's back, ending the gentle phase of the kiss and moving to something more. Casey responded to Iris's impatience with a sense of urgency of her own, opening her mouth at the first touch of Iris's tongue. Casey's fingers, which had been moving with teasing slowness through her hair, now gripped her low on her hips, pulling her close with a gentle shifting movement.

Iris became fluid. Wet with desire, pliable with an aching need to be closer. Hot and damp everywhere her skin touched Casey's. Not enough skin. She wanted more.

Casey stopped the kiss with a gasping breath, as if breaking the surface of the water for a gulp of air. She took Iris's hand and tugged her along, over the baby gate and down the hall to the other bedroom. Iris caught up to her from behind, sliding her arms around Casey's waist and holding Casey's back tightly against her front. She felt every shift Casey made, every hitched breath she took.

"Payback," Iris whispered before she took Casey's earlobe between her teeth and nibbled gently. She switched to the same slow motion Casey had used to drive her insane moments before. A trail of tiny bites and licks down the side of her neck to the top of her collarbone. A slow grind of her hips against Casey's. A tantalizingly unhurried foray under the hem of Casey's shirt, along her ribcage, and to her breast.

Iris thought she had felt empowered when she controlled the aircraft, but it couldn't compare to how she felt now. Casey's breath came in shuddering waves, and she dropped her head back onto Iris's shoulder, opening herself to Iris's mouth. Her skin shivered everywhere Iris touched her, from her taut stomach muscles to her hard nipples. Iris couldn't go slowly any longer, even if she wanted to. She kept one hand on Casey's breast, kneading in rhythm with the urgent motion of her hips, and unbuttoned Casey's jeans with the other. She slid her hand between rough denim and soft skin, reveling in the way the material pressed her close to Casey. Casey was wet and hard and ready, and Iris felt her orgasm along the entire length of her body, as if it was originating inside her.

Iris relaxed her hold enough for them to move together to the bed and lie down on top of the quilt. She didn't have time to catch her breath before Casey was straddling her, brushing her hair off her damp forehead and dropping soft kisses over her eyebrows, her temples, and the corners of her mouth. Iris strained toward her, but Casey had already moved on and was kissing her neck, between her breasts, along her stomach.

Iris closed her eyes, focusing on the sensations Casey was creating every place her hands or mouth touched her. A tug on the waistband of her jeans echoed through Iris's belly. Strong hands pressed her thighs open, and Iris felt Casey's breath against her, sending a small chill through her body and making her nipples harden in response. Almost immediately, the coolness was replaced by the burning heat of Casey's mouth and tongue. Iris cried out from the sheer pleasure of feeling Casey licking and sucking her as her hips moved against the textured fabric of the quilt. Iris called out Casey's name as she came, spiraling out of control before dropping into a steady pulse. She reached out weak arms for Casey, and held her close.

Chapter Eighteen

Casey resisted the insistent pull of sleep. She felt Iris relax in her arms, and she kissed her temple, lingering close to the floral and vanilla scent of her hair as if it was a shield designed to protect them in this space. What was beyond it? Jobs and responsibilities. Good-byes and letting go.

This day—and this whole time on the islands—had been alternately painful and joyful for Casey. She had worked hard for years to keep memories away and to avoid reflecting on anything but scientific theorems and questions. But here with Iris, on San Juan, she had let some of the past resurface. The memories hurt, as she had expected, but they also made her feel closer to whole than she had felt before. She had been a jigsaw puzzle with missing pieces, and the memories patched those blank spots with sadness, but also with the colors and shapes that made her who she was.

The memories had begun as soon as she'd stepped off the ferry, but she would have managed to ignore them as usual if Iris hadn't been there to ask questions, to share her own past, and to validate Casey's old anger and sorrow. She kissed Iris again, rubbing her fingers through Iris's hair and along the curve of her neck, over and over with varying degrees of pressure. Iris's body responded to every subtle change in touch. She shivered at a delicate tickle of fingernails and moaned and curved closer at a stronger touch. Casey wanted to learn everything about Iris, starting first and foremost with her body's needs and desires.

Casey's hand stilled, and Iris raised her head and propped her chin on Casey's chest. "What are you thinking?" she asked.

"Just that this feels good. Right now, exactly like it is." Casey didn't have to say anything else because she saw a sadness in Iris's expression that must be a reflection of her own. The second half of her explanation hung silently between them—*yes, this is good, but it's going to change. It has to change.*

But not immediately. Casey resumed her exploration of Iris's responses, categorizing them in her mind. If she rubbed the back of her knuckles over the soft swell of Iris's breast, then Iris sighed and slid her leg between Casey's thighs. If she held a tight nipple between her thumb and finger, tugging gently, then Iris gasped and pressed her hip against Casey, putting pressure on her reawakening clit. Casey decided Option B was worth a more in-depth study, especially since she discovered a direct correlation between the movement of her fingers and the corresponding pressure from Iris's hips.

"You've inspired me," Iris said haltingly, her breath coming more rapidly the more Casey teased her nipple.

"To do what?" Casey asked. She felt breathless as well, wet and heavy with a need to come, and she raised up on one elbow to allow Iris better access to her.

"New line of greeting cards," Iris said, apparently unable to form complete sentences anymore.

Casey let go of Iris's breast and moved her hand lower, closing her eyes in pleasure when she felt how wet Iris was. "About rocks?"

Iris laughed. "Not the puns again. *Thank you for great sex* cards."

"Geology themes would sell better. Mention *original horizontality*," Casey suggested. She moved her fingers in a waving motion against Iris's clit and smiled when Iris's hips jolted against her in response. "Or *oscillation ripples*. Something ought to rhyme with that."

"How about a *Please make me come* card?"

"I'll send a response to the last one right away." Casey matched the rhythm of her hips against Iris's with the rapid movement of her fingers, watching as Iris bit her lip and closed her eyes before crying out and shuddering against Casey's hand, setting off a chain reaction inside Casey that made her come for Iris. Because of her. *With* her.

❖

Iris wanted to stay in bed forever, but she had a shelter full of animals to feed. Leo would take care of the job if she wasn't out there at dinnertime, but Iris needed to get to work. She was already feeling the loss of Casey even though she was holding her in a tight embrace. Iris had been able to ignore it before, when her body's needs overruled any thoughts her brain might have had, but her mind reasserted itself now. Soon—hopefully two or three or more nights away—Casey would go. Iris would still be here, so she needed to be here completely now.

"Feeding time," Casey said in a drowsy voice.

Iris kissed the top of her head. "You stay here. I'll take care of the animals and come back."

Casey raised up on her elbows. "I'm not taking a nap while you work. I'll help, and we'll be done sooner. And that means we'll be back in bed sooner." She pulled herself and Iris to an upright position.

They got their clothes back in order and went outside with Chert following right behind. The cold evening air was welcome against overheated skin at first, but soon Iris felt goose bumps forming on her arms. She rubbed them briskly and quickened her pace, ready to be back inside the warm bungalow.

Casey knew the routine by now, and the two of them divided the chores without needing to speak. Iris was pulling the hose around the corner when she heard a vehicle in the parking lot. Casey was feeding the dogs in the infirmary, so Iris went out to see who was there.

She saw a young couple getting out of a silver minivan, and she met them halfway across the lot. Her heart jumped. Did they want to adopt? Were they looking for a lost pet? The woman was moving stiffly, holding the man's arm for support.

"Are you Iris?" he asked with a hopeful tone in his voice.

"Yes," she said, shaking hands with the man as he introduced himself as Grayson and his wife as Alice. "How can I help you?"

"We've been missing our dog since the earthquake," Grayson said with a catch in his voice. "We were in town and Alice went into labor when the quake hit. She wasn't due for another two months." He put his arm around her shoulders, and Iris could see days of stress and fear etched on their faces. "She had to be medevaced to Swedish in Seattle. I went with her, but I came back as soon as I could get on a ferry the next day to get our dog. He had gotten out of the yard. I looked for hours, but I had to get back to the hospital."

"We weren't able to leave with the baby until today," Alice continued the story. "We've been calling the humane society, but they're understaffed and barely answer their phones. Once we got back to the island and asked around, your name came up."

"We didn't mean to leave him," Grayson said. Iris clearly saw how guilty they both felt. Alice didn't look like she should be on her feet, let alone driving around to shelters.

"I understand. I'm just glad your baby and you are okay. Can you describe your dog? Do you have pictures?"

"Gibson is a male golden retriever, almost five years old," Grayson said. He pulled out his phone and scrolled through before handing it to her.

Iris stared at the picture and felt as weak as Alice looked. She'd had her suspicions from the start, but had hoped she was wrong. She hated hoping *against* one of her dogs finding its home, but she did this time.

"He was in the woods near Lime Kiln, trapped in an old fishing net," Iris said. "He was unable to get free, but a friend of mine cut him loose."

"You have him? He's here?" Alice's face folded into tears.

"Yes. Can you give me a minute? I'll bring him out here to you."

They nodded and stayed put although she could see they were eager to get to their dog. Iris walked back to the kennels with pain in every step. She wanted another way out, but what could she do? Tell Casey to grab Chert and run out the back? The wonder of their day together, the joy of touching Casey, all of it faded into the background and was replaced by a hollow ache inside. How much worse would it be for Casey?

Iris found her near the back of the kennels, filling the rest of the water bowls. She turned at the sound of Iris's approach, and Iris watched her expression shift as she figured out the situation as if Iris had the actual story written on her face. Happiness, concern, realization followed in quick succession on Casey's. She glanced at Chert who was smiling at them, joyfully unaware of any drama taking place.

"They're here," Casey said.

"Yes. Oh, Casey, I'm sorry." Iris felt tears running down her own cheeks even though Casey's were dry. "If there was something I could do…"

"Why…" Casey cleared her throat with a shallow sound. "Why did it take them so long to find him? Why did they leave him?"

"The wife went into labor during the earthquake. Premature. They had to go to the mainland."

Casey nodded as if accepting the explanation, but Iris kept talking.

"They tried, Casey. They didn't mean to abandon him."

"Well, it's good. For him to go back home. I should…I need to go inside, Iris."

She looked at the water hose she was holding as if uncertain how it had gotten in her hand. Iris walked over and took it from her, holding Casey's chin and making her look up. "Go back to the bungalow. I'll take care of this and be right there."

Casey gave her a hard, desperate kiss on the mouth, and then knelt to hug Chert tightly around his neck. Then she stood up and walked away.

Iris watched her go, sensing a finality to Casey's good-bye. Chert started to follow Casey as usual, but Iris whistled for him and he obediently came back. She took him out to the family, praying desperately that they would say she had the wrong dog, but the tremor she felt run through him when he saw his family dispelled all hope that he wasn't theirs. She watched the reunion with a detachment that was unusual for her. She always felt a flow of emotions when a dog left her shelter—sadness and happiness blended into one powerful singularity—but she only felt as numb as Casey had looked when she heard the news.

Iris forced herself to work methodically through her out-take process, not wanting her dazed state to get in the way of making sure everything was in order. She had to admit to herself that she was avoiding going back to the bungalow and facing Casey. She had a bunch of platitudes and greeting card snippets in her head, but nothing to help Casey handle the pain of losing her dog and companion. She had a feeling the experience would be even more intense for Casey because she had fought so hard to pretend that she was logical and unemotional.

Finally, though, the family left. Agatha and Leo had been watching the events from the back of the kennels, and they came out as soon as the car was gone.

"I...I'll finish feeding and go talk to her." Iris stumbled over the words. What would she say? Was there anything that would get through to Casey?

"Go. Be with her." Agatha turned her toward the bungalow and gave her a push. "We'll finish out here."

Iris nodded and kept walking, as if Agatha's push had given her just enough strength to make it to the door of the bungalow. It was ajar, and she went inside, unsure if she would find Casey there or if she had already left.

She was still there, but her suitcase was on the mussed bed. Iris had to turn away from the scene of their lovemaking—was it really only an hour ago that they had been there, playfully pretending they could ignore the outside world? It felt like weeks had passed between then and now. Iris left the room and went into the back bedroom, where Casey was sitting next to the box of kittens. She had her knees pulled against her chest, and she was watching the kittens without touching them.

Iris sat on the bed and let the silence stretch between them for a few minutes.

"I have to go, Iris," Casey said. Her voice sounded scratchy, as if she had been crying, but her eyes were dry and distant.

"You don't have to. You're choosing to go." Iris felt the numbness that had paralyzed her heart vanish at Casey's words. The resulting rush of emotions, of desperation and pain, felt like a physical wave hit her. She braced her hands on either side of her as if anchoring herself to the bed, to this place.

"You don't understand." Casey turned and looked at her. "It's not just having him leave. That's survivable because he's going home. But if I feel this horrible losing him, how can I handle losing you?"

Casey winced every time she referred to Chert, obviously trying to downplay the pain she was feeling, but Iris could tell she meant every word of her final sentence.

"That's the choice you're making. The decision was made for you with Chert, but not with me. I love you, Casey. We could try to find some way…"

Even as she spoke the words, Iris heard the arguments against her suggestion in her mind. She didn't want to admit to them, but Casey spoke them out loud.

"Would you be willing to leave the shelter and the animals that depend on you and move to Seattle? I couldn't live with myself if I asked you to leave your home, but I can't give up my life and move here."

"We could try long-distance. Wait and see if a solution comes up."

Casey shook her head. "You know it wouldn't work. And I don't know what I'd do if I heard the news that you'd found someone else, someone who lives here and can truly share your life."

"So you're giving up? Because you might get hurt?"

Casey nodded, not rising to the angry challenge in Iris's voice. "Exactly. I should have done the same thing with the dog. Dropped him off here and not let myself get attached."

Iris stood up, too frustrated to sit still any longer. "Do you regret the time you shared with him? With me?"

Casey sat still, with barely discernible and unreadable emotions flickering in her expression. "No," she said quietly. "I'll never forget you, Iris. Living here, working with you. What we shared this afternoon. But the longer we let this go on, the harder it will be when it's time to separate. It makes sense to end things now instead of later."

"None of what you're saying makes sense," Iris said. "And you *will* forget me, just like you forgot your mom and your childhood. I'll be pushed out of your mind with work and numbers until I'm only a memory that feels more like a dream than someone real."

Iris saw Casey cringe when she mentioned her mother, and even in her anger she wanted to comfort her, to help her figure out a way to come out of hiding and let herself feel love. But she kept her distance. Casey had left her already, Iris felt it. Nothing Iris said would bring her back, and only Casey could make the choice to return.

Iris waited, but Casey made no move toward her, physically or emotionally. "Good-bye, Casey," she said quietly, and left the bungalow.

Chapter Nineteen

B lack, squiggly lines marked the seismogram. Casey stared at it as the smaller P waves became larger S waves, holding her breath until the frantic scratching of ink settled again. One point eight. Most likely, Iris hadn't even noticed the earth trembling beneath her feet. Chert might have been nervous, though, barking in the shrill tone he reserved for stressful moments. Casey turned away from the instruments. She spent way too much time observing the island through the medium of a seismometer, like she was watching some strange geologic version of a nanny cam.

She sat at her desk and started going over the miles of printouts that were curled like a scroll and covering the length of her work space. It wasn't the same as hiking along a fault line or examining intrusions of igneous rock in person, but it kept her busy. Busy was good. Distraction had become harder to maintain these days, in the two weeks since she had left Iris and the San Juans behind.

Her boss had been impressed by the observations she had made in the field and not so thrilled by the extended amount of time she had stayed there. Luckily, the quality of the former had been enough to erase any annoyance over the latter. Since then, Casey had found her place on the team here at the lab. He often asked her to join brainstorming sessions, and coworkers had gotten in the habit of bringing questionable data to her for help figuring it out. She worked hard, came in early, and stayed late. The model employee.

She hadn't slept much the night before, and the charts in front of her began to resemble Rorschach tests. The wiggly marks morphed into images of Iris and the shelter.

Here was Iris, naked in bed.

This one looked like Chert, wrapped tightly in the snare of a fishing net.

Here was Leo, stealthily moving through the kennels. Jazz, cooking something deep-fried and delicious in her pub's kitchen.

Casey shoved the readouts away from her and went into the break room. The lab was sterile compared to the grungy process of forging trails through the woods and scrabbling over huge boulders, but she brought all the untidy elements of the islands to work with her in her mind. She poured some bottled water into a mug and put it in the microwave, wincing at the odor of too many nuked meals. She needed to adjust to life back on the mainland, and she needed to do it fast.

When the microwave beeped, she took out the mug and added a packet of instant oatmeal, stirring as the less-disgusting aroma of artificial cinnamon replaced the miscellaneous and unappetizing food smells. She sat at a Formica table and looked outside. The view was beautiful here, with plenty of green space and Lake Washington in the background. On a clear day, she'd be able to see the Cascades and Mount Rainier. She smiled, thinking of her day with Iris on Orcas Island and remembering their jokes about the mythical, cloud-covered mountains of Washington State.

Casey had thought about calling Iris at least a hundred times a day. Like the seismic events she studied, her urges to make contact were sometimes manageable and sometimes overpowering in magnitude. She resisted, though, but her reasons why became less distinct and convincing as time passed.

All she had to do to get back on track, though, was to remember the way her heart broke when she saw Iris's face that last evening she spent at the shelter. She saw Iris's sadness when she came to break the news about Chert, but there had been something else in her expression. Something resolute and accepting. This was the way her shelter worked, something she must experience all the time. She got close to the animals, but she had to let them go. Iris didn't believe she was a brave person, but she was wrong. She could handle the pain of saying good-bye, but Casey couldn't.

Casey saw the wind moving the needle-covered branches of a large pine tree, and she almost felt the same breeze in her hair and brushing across her face, bringing with it the sweet smell of sap and the tang of the ocean. She shook her head. She was inside the lab, surrounded by metal and plastic, and eating the shreds of cardboard that were supposed to be oats. Her senses had been reawakened on the island, and sometimes she felt invigorated by them. Other times, she felt as if she had gone back to sleepwalking since her return.

She rinsed her mug and went back to her desk and unrolled the readouts again. Interpreting blips and marks on computer printouts wasn't the same as reading the earth itself, but she was paid to study data and not to wander through nature, rhapsodizing about rocks. She spent the next three hours dutifully marking up the scroll with notes. When she couldn't stand it any longer, she rolled the printout tightly and secured it with a rubber band. She'd go over the rest of it tonight.

Casey caught the bus, relieved not to have to drive through heavy Seattle traffic, and got off a stop before the one for her apartment. She walked two blocks down the hill toward the Sound and entered the bustling streets of Pike Place Market. Every time she came here, she pictured Iris wandering happily from stall to stall, tasting samples and buying whatever ingredients caught her creative fancy. Iris was always *here*, no matter where Casey went, but she was especially present in the colorful and aromatic market. Still, Casey chose to come here instead of going to a less Iris-like grocery store.

She took out her list and checked off items as she bought them. A small bunch of fresh oregano, some carrots, celery, a packet of freshly made egg noodles. She took her small bag, trying not to count how many people had dogs with them in the market, and walked the remaining blocks to her apartment.

She set the messenger bag containing the printout scroll and other work she had brought home on the hallway floor and went into her tiny galley kitchen. She had been attempting to bring some of the island home with her, to assuage the pain she had felt when she left everything behind. Her plan had been to learn to cook, as if the homemade food she had eaten there had been the big draw. She was having fun following recipes and studying the scientific principles of the culinary arts, but the results only made her miss Iris even more.

Maybe someday she'd get past it and eat a meal in her own place without being transported back to the San Juans and Iris. Not today apparently, but someday. She placed her tablet on the counter and carefully followed the directions for making soup. She wasn't as skilled as Iris yet, but she studied hard—another way to keep her mind busy—and she was learning.

She took out a ruler and marked the optimum thickness of a carrot slice before cutting the vegetable into uniform coins.

Celery followed, in neat U-shaped segments. The oregano was more challenging. She peeled the tiny leaves off the stalks with no problem, but she had to search for an online video before she figured out what exactly a rough chop meant.

Casey ran her knife over the herb, releasing a pungent, earthy scent. She could too easily imagine Iris in the kitchen with her, laughing at Casey's obsessiveness about using rulers and instructional videos. Casey would insist that her way was better, with measurable results and a clear adherence to the recipe's instructions. A playful wrestling match for control over the ingredients would ensue, followed by a not-so-playful kiss that would make them forget about cooking and head into the bedroom. Or onto the kitchen floor...

"Damn!" Casey nicked her finger with the knife and hurried into the bathroom for some ointment and a Band-Aid. She came back into the kitchen and cleaned off her cutting board, getting a fresh handful of oregano and starting over with the process of cutting it. She needed to focus, or she'd burn down her whole building.

Once she had the broth simmering with vegetables, noodles, and oregano, a warm and homey smell permeated the apartment. She got a packet of crackers out of the cabinet—Iris wouldn't have made them from scratch, would she?—and set the table with a single bowl and spoon. That looked much too sad, so she got a tray instead, and set it next to a chair in the living room. She ate her meal in there, with the noise of the television providing a distracting background. The food was good, and she was improving in her abilities. Iris would have been proud, complimenting her on the soup and making plans for teaching her something new and more challenging.

Casey sighed and pushed the empty bowl away. She couldn't even eat a meal in peace, without memories of Iris haunting her. She cleaned up the kitchen and got out her computer. She'd try to work Iris right out of her mind.

She had already finished her paper, but she hadn't stopped writing. She still had a few scraps of paper from her time on the island. On them were scrawled her own words, written by both Iris and herself, from the times when she had gotten carried away with her excitement about the geological marvels around them. She had started wondering if she could share her fascination with other people, not just other geologists. Iris had been inspired enough by Casey's words to write a poem. Maybe other readers would be inspired to see the world around them in a new way if they understood some of the wonders on which they stood and walked and lived.

Casey wrote for over an hour before she saved her work and turned off the computer. She should thank Iris somehow for inspiring this project. Casey wasn't sure where it would lead, but she loved working on it. She never would have come up with this idea if she hadn't met Iris.

She picked up the phone, wondering if she should call. Say hello, ask about the Twins and the kittens, Leo and Agatha. Instead, she found herself calling her father and waiting nervously for him to answer. It was two hours later in Chicago, but he was a night owl and wouldn't go to bed for hours.

"Hello, Casey," he said.

"Hi, Dad. How are you?" She rolled her eyes at the inane beginning to the conversation, and from the tone of his voice she figured he was doing the same thing. They weren't the type of family to call and share small talk or bits of news about their days, but he played along. They covered her grandparents' health—good—and the weather—bad—before she got to the question she wanted to ask.

"I've been thinking. About Mom. What she looked like, stuff like that." Her words sounded stilted because she had to force them out. "Do you have any pictures of her?"

He was silent for a moment. "We kept some things, pictures and some personal items. I'll have your grandmother send the box."

Casey was relieved to have *something*. She felt a surge of anger, though, since she hadn't been told these items existed before now. Of course, she hadn't asked about them, either. This was yet another way her life had changed because of Iris and because of her time on the island. She had gotten accustomed to having memories of her mother near, and she had gradually started to hoard them like treasures instead of pushing them away with other less emotion-laden thoughts.

"Thank you. I've been thinking of her, and about when I first came to live with you." Casey hesitated. She needed answers because she couldn't conjure up certain memories on her own, but for some reason she was afraid to ask. Because she didn't think her dad would want to talk about the past? Or for some other reason?

"You know how I was on the San Juan Islands after the earthquake? Most of the hotels were closed, so I ended up staying at an animal rescue place. I liked being around the dogs."

"Okay." He drew the syllables out until they sounded like a question.

"I remember wanting one when I was little." Casey just made the statement. She couldn't ask the questions. *Why didn't you let me get one? Why did you deny me the company and comfort of a pet?*

She heard his sigh over the phone. "We couldn't keep her, Casey. Both your grandparents and I worked full time, and you were in school. I know you missed her, but you got over it just fine."

At first, Casey thought he was talking about her mother, and then a rush of memories returned, making her gasp out loud.

"I had a dog. *We* did. Mom and I." An image of a little hairy dog with black fur and floppy ears filled her mind. Running to greet her. Playing in the backyard. *Her* dog. She had been crying for her own pet, not because she wanted them to get her a new one.

"Yes. Isn't that what you're talking about? Anyway, the past is in the past."

Casey somehow managed to get through their good-byes and end the call. She sat in shocked silence for a long time, with tears falling down her cheeks. She still didn't have much recall from those early years, but some parts were there. She hadn't lost everything. Thanks to Iris and her animals.

Everything was in turmoil in Casey's mind, as if the world had shifted and the theories she had formed about the world were based on incorrect and incomplete data. She knew one fact with absolute certainty and with all her heart, though. Her mother would have loved Iris. Because of the person she was, yes. But mostly because Casey was in love with her.

She had lost too much over the years. It was time to stop pushing love and life away just because it might get messy and painful.

Chapter Twenty

Iris sat in her folding chair with the Twins curled at her feet, contentedly chewing their cud. She finished one last greeting card and tucked her notepad between her seat and the armrest, stretching her legs out in front of her. She had been sitting here for hours—long enough for the Twins to get tired of playing keep-away with her colored pencils and for her muscles to begin to protest about the unsupportive chair.

She had been writing more than usual since Casey left. Mostly *thinking of you* cards. Every time she was tempted to call her or send an email, she wrote down a verse instead, added an illustration that had nothing to do with her or Casey or the time they had spent together, and mailed it to one of her publishers instead of delivering it to Casey.

She hoped that writing down the words of loneliness would eventually leave her devoid of them, but she seemed to have an inexhaustible supply. Casey was everywhere around here. She'd left traces of herself in every kennel panel she had repaired and every fence board she had replaced. She was in the bungalow, where the kittens played and slept. She was in the kennel office, where she and Leo had shared morning coffee and philosophical discussions.

Most of all, she was on Iris's skin. Everywhere she had touched was branded now, as if her fingers had inked tattoos across Iris's chest, between her thighs, and along her cheek-bones. In bed at night, Iris would replay their single time together, and she still felt the heated trail of Casey's hands and mouth on her.

She flipped to a blank page, and a poem tumbled from her fantasies and across the white paper. She could feel her skin flush as she wrote. This one was far too erotic for a grocery aisle greeting card, but she had a smile playing around the corners of her mouth as she wrote, even though she was a little embarrassed by the words and phrases she was using.

When she was finished, she tore the sheet from her notepad and folded it before tucking it in the pocket of her jeans. This one was just for her, and she didn't want to risk leaving her notepad lying around and having someone else read it.

She leaned back again and closed her eyes. Getting her feelings on the page was cathartic for a brief moment, but she knew the pain and emptiness would come rushing back once she was done. She missed Casey, plain and simple. The sex had been amazing, and Casey's body excited her beyond any lover she had ever known before, but the longing went far deeper. She wanted to sit at a café with Casey, go on a walk, or clean the kennels. All the small, everyday events they had shared while she was here.

Casey was air to her, filling in all the corners of her life. When she had gone, Iris's world had collapsed.

On the inside, that is. On the outside, she was changed in a different way by Casey. She had expanded, even though her daily life seemed pretty much the same on the surface. She wanted to share these transformations with Casey, but she couldn't.

She picked up her notepad and folded her chair, carefully stepping around the little goats as she headed back to the office.

She stowed her chair behind the desk and went back to her house.

Casey would be proud to know that Iris had sent some poems to a literary magazine. The submission had included three of the ones Iris had stuffed in her file cabinet long ago, plus a couple she had written while thinking of something Casey had said or done. She sent the latter ones mainly to get the damned things out of the house because every line, every word was full of memories.

Iris went inside and washed her hands at the kitchen sink. She started pulling ingredients out of the fridge and pantry, setting up her familiar meal-cooking assembly line. She chopped marjoram and parsley and put the fresh, bitter greens in a small glass bowl. Onions and garlic were next, overpowering every other scent in the kitchen. Iris popped a Kalamata olive in her mouth and chewed with her mouth watering at its salty bitterness while she sliced the rest of them into uneven chunks. She zested and juiced several lemons as well.

Once everything was prepped and arrayed in front of her, she began to cook the chicken for her Greek dish. She had chosen this recipe because she knew Casey would have loved the powerful flavors that were offset by the citrus notes of the lemon. Casey wouldn't be here to enjoy it, of course, but Iris liked imagining her standing by the counter and stealing bites of food from the bowls.

Once the chicken and onions were browned, Iris added some broth and the rest of the ingredients and put the casserole dish in the oven. Soon the whole house would smell like a Greek diner. Iris smiled and put the finishing touches on the dining room table while she waited for people to arrive. This meal wouldn't be going into the freezer, but would be enjoyed tonight. Another example of Casey's influence on her.

She put bowls and crumbly feta and fresh parsley on the table. Jazz would be bringing salad and baklava to complete the meal. Instead of packing away food for a just-in-case emergency, Iris would be sharing what she had prepared with Leo and Agatha, Jazz, and Sean and his wife.

Iris got in the shower, ever mindful of Casey's absence. She and Casey would have had fun tonight, planning a meal for friends and sharing the evening with them. And once everyone had left, they would have had their own party, just the two of them, celebrating each other.

Iris shut off the water and hugged her towel to her damp body. She wasn't only missing Casey, but she was mourning the loss of what they could have been. She had to pull herself together and get on with her life. She couldn't be like her parents, living every moment with the hollowness of a ghost next to them.

Iris sat on her bed, still naked, and faced what she had to do. She claimed she lived in the present, but her childhood had made her adopt the philosophy—or excuse—of not expecting more or hoping for more. She needed to break the pattern, and the loss of Casey was the catastrophe she needed to make her do so.

She peeked at the past with one of those sideways glances of the mind, not prepared to face everything head-on, but ready to start. Her childhood was what it was, and she'd never be able to change it. When she looked further along, at her college days and her decision to move to the island, she found herself looking with Casey's eyes. The choice to come here might have presented itself without her actively searching for it, but she had made the gutsy move of jumping on the opportunity. Even though she had often lamented her lack of ambition to go far and do more, she had, as Casey put it, *gone deep*. She had no regrets about coming to the shelter and no desire to leave for more than a vacation at a time.

And the future? She had equated hope with unhappiness somehow. If she looked for more, it meant she wasn't satisfied with what she had. Could she accept the idea of having dreams and still being happy where she was? She thought so. Her poems were winging their way across the country now, carrying the secret hope that they'd be valued by others. And if they weren't? She could live with that, too.

Iris got off the bed and finished drying herself. She chose a pair of comfortable slacks and a purple shell and cardigan combination and put them on. As far as love went, she was going to have to live in the past a little longer. What she had with Casey was too much, too wonderful, too beautiful to forget right away. They hadn't spent much time together in terms of hours and weeks, but they had, in their own way, gone deep there as well.

Iris would keep the memories, live with the sadness as long as she needed to, and then she'd move forward. She wasn't sure what direction she would take, but she wanted to feel love again. Maybe Casey would be ready eventually...

Maybe, maybe. Iris had avoided maybes all her life, but now she welcomed the relief they gave. The short word was long on hope.

She heard a knock at the door and stepped out of her introspective mood and into the role of host and friend. Jazz came first, filling the house with as much flavor and brightness as the scent of Iris's cooking. Iris couldn't possibly be mopey around her for long. Sean and Jeannette came soon after, and once Leo and Agatha saw the cars arriving, they'd made the short trip from their own house.

Iris got everyone drinks, and then went into the kitchen to check the chicken. She turned away from the oven and gave a shriek of surprise to find Leo standing directly behind her.

He laughed. "I did that one on purpose," he said.

"Seriously, I'm getting that cat bell," Iris warned him, but she laughed as she spoke. Her expressions whenever he snuck up on her must be amusing.

His voice changed to a more serious tone. "How are you, Iris?"

She shrugged. Normally, she would have answered with a dismissive phrase to prove she was untouched by what had happened. *Fine. Doing great, thanks!* "I miss her, Leo," she said instead. "All the time. But I'll get better."

"Of course you will. She already made you better in some ways, too, even though she wasn't here long."

Iris thought about her poems and listened to the laughter coming from the living room. "Yes, she did."

He gave her shoulder a squeeze and left the kitchen. Iris barely had time to check the roasting potatoes, fragrant with bright olive oil and herbs, before Jazz had taken his place.

"Are you going to ask how I'm doing, too?" Iris asked, spearing a potato with a fork to check its tenderness. "Tonight's answer is I'm sad, but I'll get better."

Jazz grinned and perched on one of the stools next to the counter. "We care about you, so be prepared to be pestered. Jeannette is next on the list to take you aside with a consoling hug and some kind words."

Iris leaned against the counter and handed Jazz the fork with the roasted potato speared on the end. "I appreciate it. It's like my greeting cards have come to life and are following me through the day, reassuring me and offering words of encouragement."

"Mm. These are delicious! If we're cards come to life, we'll have to start speaking in verse," Jazz said. She cleared her throat and spoke in a booming voice. "Roses are red, violets are lazy, find someone else, and forget about Casey."

Iris laughed at the silly words, but Jazz must have seen her heart breaking at the same time. She got up and hugged her tightly, squeezing the breath right out of her. "I'm teasing, darling. In a way. You will find someone because you're too great a catch to be alone. I have some ideas in mind once you're ready to move on. Or maybe you hope she'll come back someday?"

Hope. "I guess I do," Iris admitted. "I want her back. Maybe someday I'll contact her again, see if she's okay, at least. And maybe, someday..."

Iris felt a lightness inside when she finished speaking. It felt good to have hope, even if it might not come true. Acknowledging it instead of letting it fester inside and make her bitter. Sharing her pain with friends instead of dealing with it alone.

"She went with me to a home check near Victoria when she was here," Iris said, watching Jazz go to the oven and snag another tiny red potato. She remembered every nuance of the day, from the taste of chutney to the sight of Casey's tense expression when Sean had her fly the plane. She especially remembered coming home to the bungalow, but she had to push those thoughts away before she turned a horrific shade of red in front of company. "The family's teenage son was grieving because his childhood pet had died the year before, and he was really struggling with the idea of having another dog in the house. Casey went out of her way to talk to him and try to help him find a way to accept the new animal."

"Did she help?" Jazz asked around a mouthful of potato.

"Yes. I brought Blackjack to his new home last week. I showed the boy, Chris, some photos of what he looked like when he first arrived at the shelter and told him how Blackjack had been treated. It's what Casey had already done—getting him to focus on the new dog and how much he needed to be loved rather than on his own feelings of guilt and grief. Blackjack went right over to him the moment we arrived, and Chris really seemed happy to have him there."

Iris got a serving bowl and put the potatoes in it before Jazz ate them all. "Casey asked me to let her know how it went when I took him to his new home, and I've been thinking of sending her a note and a picture I took of the family. Chris has a big smile on his face, and Blackjack is right at his side."

Jazz smiled. "I remember the first day she came, looking kind of huffy about being on the island and having all the hotels closed. She was closed, too. Hurting. This place was good for her, but mostly it was you who healed her. She just needs some time to realize she can be happy, because it scares her, just like it did for that young Chris."

Iris nodded. She'd give Casey time, and then she'd try to get back in contact with her. If nothing worked, she'd move on, but she had to at least give her relationship with Casey one more chance. And maybe Casey would eventually be ready to be with Iris.

Maybe.

Chapter Twenty-one

Casey stood near the railing as the ferry left the last dock before heading to San Juan Island. The wind tousled her hair, but she had managed to make the time to get it cut before coming here. Every once in a while, she caught herself swiping at her bangs even though they were no longer in her eyes.

She had changed in more ways than the length of her hair since the last time she had been on one of these ferries. Then, she had stayed in her truck, rocking slightly as she'd tried to press down the grief she felt after having Chert torn away from her. And from tearing herself away from Iris. Life was going to be painful sometimes, but she didn't have to make it worse by refusing to form any attachments at all. She'd learned the lesson the hard way, during nights spent thinking about how much it would have comforted the child-Casey to have been able to keep her dog, some small part of her mother.

When Casey had first come to the island to study the effects of the quake, she had fought to keep detached from the beauty around her and from the fiery Iris. She had been coming here to observe. To stand outside and look in. She had been heading into exile, but now she hoped she was heading home.

The ferry slowed as it entered the harbor, and Casey took one last look around before heading to her truck. The scenery looked the same, with white specks of gulls floating on the surface of the water and hovering in the air as they made wind currents visible. The water was the same blue-gray it would be until the weather shifted and the near-constant cloud cover blew away. The smells of diesel and salty air vied for dominance, and the fuel was winning as the engines churned and fought to keep the ferry at a slow pace. Even from a distance, though, Casey noticed a major difference in the harbor.

People. Everywhere she looked. Families stood along the pier, with children bundled in thick coats and wrapped in scarves. Pedestrians were moving up and down the hill leading away from the dock, their movements chaotic and unpredictable as they darted in and out of buildings. Casey had come to love the quiet atmosphere of the post-earthquake San Juan Island, but she appreciated what she was seeing now even more because she understood what the revival of tourism meant for Jazz and the other business owners in town.

Casey got in her truck and drove off the ferry, passing a long line of waiting cars as she left the water behind and headed inland. She went by the Thai fusion place and decided she would take Iris there sometime. If Iris forgave her, of course.

Casey didn't like contemplating what a huge *if* led that sentence. She had turned her back on Iris, and Iris had every right to be angry. Casey would do whatever it took, for however long it took, to get Iris to forgive her. She'd start right away, with an apology and as much of an explanation as Iris would be willing to hear. She needed Iris in her life.

Casey headed directly to the shelter and parked at the edge of the lot, near the main road. She didn't want to see anyone but

Iris yet, until they had a chance to talk, so she parked out of the line of sight of Leo, Agatha, and the kennels. Iris's car wasn't in its usual parking spot, but Casey knocked on the door anyway, anxious to see her. She paced along the front walk for about ten minutes before she decided to go to the bungalow. She fished the spare key out of the hanging basket by the porch and let herself in.

She stood in the hallway and blinked to let her eyes adjust to the lighting and to give herself time to pull herself together again. There was no Chert to come running to her side with a floppy-tongued smile. The scent of Iris's cooking was gone, as was the faint hint of sweet smokiness from nightly fires and the more pungent odor of Chert baking the wetness from the sea out of his furry coat. Casey blinked back tears. She still felt the hollowness inside when she thought of the dog, but this time she wanted to run to Iris for comfort. Not away from her.

She finally was able to walk deeper into the house. The baby gate was still in place, but it had been covered with a piece of cardboard, presumably to keep kittens from slipping between the slats and escaping from the room. Casey stepped over the gate and went to the closet, where the gray cat surprised her by getting up from the cushy blanket and coming over to her, rubbing against her calves and purring in her loud, mechanical-sounding way. Casey knelt to pet her, and then she turned her attention to the kittens.

They were swarming around the closet with staggering gaits and bright open eyes. Casey tentatively reached out to pet the little calico. The kitten purred in response, with a sound that seemed too loud for her tiny body to produce, and she tripped over the edge of the carpet in her attempt to get closer to Casey. She picked her up and held her carefully against her body with both hands, rubbing her cheek against the warm fur with a sigh.

"What are you doing here, Casey?"

Iris's voice made her jump. She must be taking stealth lessons from Leo. Casey put the kitten gently back with her brothers and sisters and stood up slowly. She heard the wariness in Iris's voice and she wanted to earn her trust again, but she suddenly forgot all the speeches she had been rehearsing over the past week while she made arrangements to return to the island. She hadn't made hotel reservations, though, because she'd hoped Iris would welcome her back here. Maybe she should have had a backup plan, because Iris didn't look ready to jump into her arms just yet.

"I should never have left."

Iris just watched her, with a neutral expression on her face. Casey would have preferred happiness, or even anger. Something besides the distant look she was receiving.

"I hadn't realized how torn up I would feel about Chert until those people came for him. I couldn't handle feeling so much, and I ran away. I'm sorry."

Iris shook her head and crossed her arms over her chest. "You hurt me, too, while you were protecting yourself. You knew you were leaving the island, and that he might have a family waiting for him. Either way, you were going to have to say good-bye to him."

Casey sighed. She seemed to be getting nowhere. She hadn't realized how selfish she had been, walking out on Iris. She might have reasons for behaving like she had, reasons she could trace back to the time when she was wrenched away from her home and sent to Chicago to live with her father, but excuses and reasons wouldn't work here.

"I don't blame you if you don't want to forgive me. But be prepared, because I'm not going away again. I'll keep hounding you until you take me back because I love you, Iris."

Her last words were spoken so quietly, she wasn't sure if Iris heard them except for the subtle shift in her expression as her eyes widened slightly and her lips parted in a look of surprise.

"You're not going away? That's going to be one hell of a commute."

Casey shook her head and brushed absently at her short bangs. "My commute is twenty minutes away. The lab has an affiliate substation on Lopez. I got the job there." Iris still didn't speak, so Casey kept talking. "It's mostly part-time, unless there's significant seismic activity, which I hope there isn't because I love you and these animals and the community here. See? Even uncaring geologists can change."

The corner of Iris's mouth quirked up in a small smile. "I don't know. What if you need extra hours one month? Will you start praying for an earthquake to study?"

Casey felt a little more optimistic at the return of Iris's playful side. She ventured a step closer. "I've got enough savings to help me through for a long time. Plus, I'm working on a project inspired by you. I can use the extra time for it."

Iris seemed to struggle internally, with her curiosity winning the battle. "What kind of project?" she eventually asked.

"I'm writing a book about geology for non-geologists. I want to capture the wonder and amazement I feel when I look at formations and can read the history of the earth in them. I want to share my passion, because I loved sharing it with you."

Iris smiled all the way. "And I loved hearing about your rocks and their stories. It's a great idea, Casey. You inspired me, too, you know. I've sent some of my poems to magazines." She shrugged. "We'll see."

Casey grinned in response, and she wasn't sure whether she felt elated because she'd had some influence on Iris, too, or because she was sensing the return of their camaraderie. She thought about how close she had come to losing her completely, just because she was too weak to handle the depth of emotion she felt between them. Never again, she vowed, would she try to escape her love for Iris.

She moved forward and put her arms around Iris, hugging her tightly. The hint of lavender in Iris's hair, the softness of her cheek as she rubbed it almost imperceptibly against Casey's, and the glorious feeling of Iris's body pressed against hers combined to wrap her in a haze of love and gratitude.

Her poet. Her beautiful, talented poet who was finally ready to risk sharing her creations with the world. "Look at you, being all hopeful for the future," she whispered into Iris's ear. "I'm proud of you."

Iris finally raised her arms and returned the hug. "I've been hoping for a lot of things, Casey. I hoped I'd hear from you again. See you again. But I never dared hope that you'd come back here to stay."

Casey stepped back because she wanted to look Iris in the eyes. "I came here for you. I want to be part of life here, on the island and in your shelter, but I am here because of you."

Iris raised her hand and stroked Casey's cheek. "And I was here, waiting for you."

She brought her other hand up and cupped Casey's face between her palms. She brushed her thumb across Casey's lower lip, making her body tremble in response. "I love you, too."

Iris kissed her then, causing explosions in Casey's body. She had been torn up by her abrupt departure from the island and from her conversation with her father. Anxious about the changes to the planned trajectory of her career. Frantic with the realization that Iris might not want her back.

The subtle movement of Iris's lips against hers and the rough wetness of Iris's tongue cleared away those negative emotions and left her filled with something unfamiliar. Joy. Pure and huge and overwhelming.

Casey felt a moment of panic as the emotion threatened to frighten her into calculations or numbers or some other sort of distraction. But then Iris was there, sliding her fingers into Casey's hair and pressing her hips against Casey's, and she stopped fighting. She let the love and happiness settle inside her without lessening them or shoving them aside. Casey rested her trembling hands against the small of Iris's back and felt herself settling into the sensation of coming home.

CHAPTER TWENTY-TWO

Iris unbuttoned her denim jacket and stretched out her legs, maximizing her exposure to the gentle late-spring sunshine. The Twins—now nearly full grown but still as rambunctious as ever—vied with her for control over her pen and notebook. She gently pushed Watson's nose away while she tried to think chilly Christmas-y thoughts. Snow and carols, TV specials and shiny snowflake-patterned wrapping paper. The rich flavors of dried fruit, nutmeg, and brandy baking together to make her favorite fruitcake. The shelter animals festively dressed in colorful fleece-lined winter blankets. Casey, waking her early on Christmas morning wearing a Santa hat and nothing else...

Iris's attention wandered, and Holmes took the opportunity to grab her notebook and pull. Iris didn't relinquish her grip, and several pages tore messily out of the book. Iris got up and ran after the goat, snatching the pages again before Holmes could swallow them. She went back to her folding chair, pushed Watson's front hooves off it, and sat down again.

A few months ago, she had briefly considered sending the Twins to a goat rescue center, hoping to find good homes for them. When she had mentioned her idea to Casey, though, she had looked at Iris with as much horror as if Iris had suggested getting rid of her precious rock collection. Iris shook her head. That had been the same Casey who complained about the Twins every time they managed to get into the bed of her truck and tried to eat her instruments. Iris had quickly dropped the subject. Apparently, the Twins were now permanent residents of the shelter, along with two of the gray cat's kittens. Casey didn't call any of these animals *hers*, even though she was the one who took care of them most of the time.

Iris hugged her notebook safely against her chest and let her thoughts wander back to this past Christmas. She and Casey had spent many evenings with friends, sharing the kinds of evenings Iris had hoped for when she had hosted her dinner party before Casey's return to the island. They had made a long-delayed and bittersweet trip to visit Chert and his family. They had spent hours in the kitchen together, while Iris tried to teach Casey how to bake.

For all her insistence that she was a scientist at heart, Casey had a definite compulsion to create. She usually deviated from recipes, adding unusual ingredients and experimenting with the methods and steps that Iris meticulously followed. Some of her attempts had been spectacular, some rather horrible.

Iris smiled and started to sketch a few of the images that captured the wonderful holiday she and Casey had spent together. A kitchen counter covered with ingredients and mixing bowls, with a checked towel tossed haphazardly across the corner. A decorated tree with presents and sleeping cats tucked underneath. A retriever happily carrying a dog bone with a big red bow on it. The poems followed, matching the future season with words of home, friends, and love.

Iris finished the last greeting card and was folding her chair when she heard Casey's truck pull into the parking area. She hurried out to meet her, with the Twins leading the way. She paused at the door to the kennels and watched Casey climb out of the truck and pull two cookies out of her jacket pocket for the goats. She was struck by the emotions she always felt when she saw Casey after even a day apart. Love and wonder, gratitude, and a physical pull toward her that had only grown stronger the more they were together.

Iris breathed a whispered *thank you*. That Casey had come to the island in the first place, and that she had come back again after running away. Iris couldn't imagine being without her, even though she couldn't really explain the difference Casey had made in her life. Iris still had the same friends, the same long work hours, the same responsibilities. But the life that had seemed not enough before was suddenly precious to Iris.

She met Casey halfway across the lot and wrapped her arms around Casey's neck, drawing her into a deep kiss. Casey's hands slid under her jacket and across her ribcage, pulling her flush against her body.

Casey pulled away a few centimeters and rested her forehead against Iris's. "Mmm. What a great welcome home," she said, her voice sounding a little breathless. "I missed you today."

"I missed you, too," Iris said. She tugged the corner of her jacket out of Watson's mouth and gave Casey another quick kiss. "How was work?"

"Good." Casey draped her arm across Iris's shoulders as they walked toward the kennels. The dogs—alerted by the crunch of gravel and their internal clocks—started to bark in anticipation of dinnertime.

"Ian and I took the boat to Matia Island and hiked one of the sandstone ridges. Most of the island is closed to the public, but I can take you over there sometime. You'd love how peaceful it is."

"It's a wildlife refuge, isn't it?" Iris asked as they started pouring kibble in dog bowls. "Did you see anything interesting?"

Casey shrugged with a sheepish expression. "Ian kept talking about all the birds he was seeing. I guess it's some sort of breeding area for them. I think he mentioned some sort of sparrow…Or was it an eagle?"

Iris laughed. "You were too busy looking at rocks to look up and see a bird, weren't you?"

Casey grinned. "Maybe. Here, I'll take Mickey's dinner."

Iris handed her the bowl without a word and watched her head down the aisle to the little terrier's run. She knew how much Casey had changed her life, making her world brighter and better, but she could see a difference in Casey, too. She was more open here on the island. To the people, the animals, and even to her past. She had been slow to get over losing Chert to his family, though, and she had ignored Agatha and Leo's attempts to find her a dog. Iris had stayed out of their pet matchmaking, but she'd had her suspicions about Mickey for some time now.

She finished doling out meals to the dogs and wandered over to where Casey was standing next to Mickey's kennel, her fingers wrapped through the chain-link diamonds. The little scruff of a dog was kindly called mixed breed on Iris's intake forms, and he had been in the shelter for three months. Casey regularly took one of the dogs with her when she did fieldwork, and Mickey had gone on more than his fair share of outings.

Iris stepped behind Casey and kissed the side of her neck, feeling Casey's answering sigh vibrate deep inside her. "What's on your mind?" Iris asked.

"I was thinking…I mean, since he doesn't seem to have anybody, and he likes the cats…" Casey paused and started again. "Well, would you mind if we kept him?"

Iris hugged Casey close. "I wouldn't mind at all. We can move him into the house in the morning." She laughed and sifted her fingers through Casey's hair. "You know, for all the loneliness and sadness we went through as kids, we seem to be doing quite a remarkable job of building a family together. A strange family, but a good one."

Casey turned in her arms and traced Iris's cheekbone with her fingertips, drawing a flush of heat to the surface everywhere she touched Iris's skin. "You're all I need. I love the friends and animals we've gathered around us, but you are what matters most to me."

Iris closed the small gap between them and kissed Casey, pressing her against the metal fence as their lips and bodies moved together with a growing hunger.

"Why don't we go back to the house now," Iris said with a sharp inhale as Casey softly bit the sensitive part of her neck where it met her collarbone. "I want to get a head start on my next set of greeting cards, and I have some ideas I'd like to run by you. I'm thinking about a line of erotic Valentine's Day cards—"

Casey laughed and grabbed her hand, pulling her toward their home before Iris could finish her sentence.

About the Author

Karis Walsh is the author of lesbian romances including Rainbow Award-winning *Harmony* and *Sea Glass Inn*, as well as a romantic intrigue series about a mounted police unit. She's a Pacific Northwest native who recently relocated to Texas with her goats. When she isn't writing, she's playing with her animals, cooking, reading, playing her viola, or hiking in the state park.

Books Available from Bold Strokes Books

Canvas for Love by Charlotte Greene. When ghosts from Amelia's past threaten to undermine their relationship, Chloé must navigate the greatest romance of her life without losing sight of who she is. (978-1-62639-944-0)

Heart Stop by Radclyffe. Two women, one with a damaged body, the other a damaged spirit, challenge each other to dare to live again. (978-1-62639-899-3)

Repercussions by Jessica L. Webb. Someone planted information in Edie Black's brain and now they want it back, but with the protection of shy former soldier Skye Kenny, Edie has a chance at life and love. (978-1-62639-925-9)

Spark by Catherine Friend. Jamie's life is turned upside down when her consciousness travels back to 1560 and lands in the body of one of Queen Elizabeth I's ladies-in-waiting...or has she totally lost her grip on reality? (978-1-62639-930-3)

Taking Sides by Kathleen Knowles. When passion and politics collide, can love survive? (978-1-62639-876-4)

Thorns of the Past by Gun Brooke. Former cop Darcy Flynn's heart broke when her career on the force ended in disgrace, but perhaps saving Sabrina Hawk's life will mend it in more ways than one. (978-1-62639-857-3)

You Make Me Tremble by Karis Walsh. Seismologist Casey Radnor comes to the San Juan Islands to study an earthquake but finds her heart shaken by passion when she meets animal rescuer Iris Mallery (978-1-62639-901-3)

Complications by MJ Williamz. Two women battle for the heart of one. (978-1-62639-769-9)

Crossing the Wide Forever by Missouri Vaun. As Cody Walsh and Lillie Ellis face the perils of the untamed West, they discover that love's uncharted frontier isn't for the weak in spirit or the faint of heart. (978-1-62639-851-1)

Fake It Till You Make It by M. Ullrich. Lies will lead to trouble, but can they lead to love? (978-1-62639-923-5)

Girls Next Door by Sandy Lowe and Stacia Seaman eds.. Bestselling romance authors tell it from the heart—sexy, romantic stories of falling for the girls next door. (978-1-62639-916-7)

Pursuit by Jackie D. The pursuit of the most dangerous terrorist in America will crack the lines of friendship and love, and not everyone will make it out under the weight of duty and service. (978-1-62639-903-7)

Shameless by Brit Ryder. Confident Emery Pearson knows exactly what she's looking for in a no-strings-attached hookup, but can a spontaneous interlude open her heart to more? (978-1-63555-006-1)

The Practitioner by Ronica Black. Sometimes love comes calling whether you're ready for it or not. (978-1-62639-948-8)

Unlikely Match by Fiona Riley. When an ambitious PR exec and her super-rich coding geek-girl client fall in love, they learn that giving something up may be the only way to have everything. (978-1-62639-891-7)

Where Love Leads by Erin McKenzie. A high school counselor and the mom of her new student bond in support of the troubled girl, never expecting deeper feelings to emerge, testing the boundaries of their relationship. (978-1-62639-991-4)

Forsaken Trust by Meredith Doench. When four women are murdered, Agent Luce Hansen must regain trust in her most valuable investigative tool—herself—to catch the killer. (978-1-62639-737-8)

Her Best Friend's Sister by Meghan O'Brien. For fifteen years, Claire Barker has nursed a massive crush on her best friend's older sister. What happens when all her wildest fantasies come true? (978-1-62639-861-0)

Letter of the Law by Carsen Taite. Will federal prosecutor Bianca Cruz take a chance at love with horse breeder Jade Vargas, whose dark family ties threaten everything Bianca has worked to protect—including her child? (978-1-62639-750-7)

New Life by Jan Gayle. Trigena and Karrie are having a baby, but the stress of becoming a mother and the impact on their relationship might be too much for Trigena. (978-1-62639-878-8)

Royal Rebel by Jenny Frame. Charity director Lennox King sees through the party girl image Princess Roza has cultivated, but will Lennox's past indiscretions and Roza's responsibilities make their love impossible? (978-1-62639-893-1)

Unbroken by Donna K. Ford. When Kayla and Jackie, two women with every reason to reject Happy Ever After, fall in love, will they have the courage to overcome their pasts and rewrite their stories? (978-1-62639-921-1)

Where the Light Glows by Dena Blake. Mel Thomas doesn't realize just how unhappy she is in her marriage until she meets Izzy Calabrese. Will she have the courage to overcome her insecurities and follow her heart? (978-1-62639-958-7)

Escape in Time by Robyn Nyx. Working in the past is hell on your future. (978-1-62639-855-9)

Forget-Me-Not by Kris Bryant. Is love worth walking away from the only life you've ever dreamed of? (978-1-62639-865-8)

Highland Fling by Anna Larner. On vacation in the Scottish Highlands, Eve Eddison falls for the enigmatic forestry officer Moira Burns, despite Eve's best friend's campaign to convince her that Moira will break her heart. (978-1-62639-853-5)

Phoenix Rising by Rebecca Harwell. As Storm's Quarry faces invasion from a powerful neighbor, a mysterious newcomer with powers equal to Nadya's challenges everything she believes about herself and her future. (978-1-62639-913-6)

Soul Survivor by I. Beacham. Sam and Joey have given up on hope, but when fate brings them together it gives them a chance to change each other's life and make dreams come true. (978-1-62639-882-5)

Strawberry Summer by Melissa Brayden. When Margaret Beringer's first love Courtney Carrington returns to their small town, she must grapple with their troubled past and fight the temptation for a very delicious future. (978-1-62639-867-2)

The Girl on the Edge of Summer by J.M. Redmann. Micky Knight accepts two cases, but neither is the easy investigation it appears. The past is never past—and young girls lead complicated, even dangerous lives. (978-1-62639-687-6)

Unknown Horizons by CJ Birch. The moment Lieutenant Alison Ash steps aboard the Persephone, she knows her life will never be the same. (978-1-62639-938-9)

You Make Me
Tremble